The firing at the gate had done its job

One of the limos was about to reach the house, still taking hits, with gunners firing back through hidden gun ports in the armored doors. On the run, Bolan saw one of Ramos's men go down, but the gunners still in service failed to notice the runner on their flank.

From twenty yards, the Executioner fired the high-explosive round and watched the sliding doors disintegrate, a smoky thunderclap erupting from the room within. He followed through, his finger on the trigger of the M-16A1, ready to respond to hostile fire.

One body lay draped across a sofa, blood soaking through a tattered sport coat. Just in front of him, a spiral staircase wound away to the second floor.

He was inside for what it was worth.

Above him, a gunner let loose with a shotgun, the blast of buckshot rattling over Bolan's head as he dived to the floor.

MACK BOLAN®

The Executioner

DON PENDLETON'S
THE EXECUTIONER®
FEATURING MACK BOLAN®

BAJA BLITZ

A GOLD EAGLE BOOK FROM
WORLDWIDE®

TORONTO • NEW YORK • LONDON
AMSTERDAM • PARIS • SYDNEY • HAMBURG
STOCKHOLM • ATHENS • TOKYO • MILAN
MADRID • WARSAW • BUDAPEST • AUCKLAND

First edition February 1993

ISBN 0-373-61170-6

Special thanks and acknowledgment to
Mike Newton for his contribution to this work.

BAJA BLITZ

Adversity is the first path to Truth.

—Lord Byron

Rightness of judgment is bitterness to the heart.

—Euripides

We have a hard road ahead of us, to find the truth, but our enemies have brought the bitter judgment on themselves. I am not their judge, I am their Executioner.

—Mack Bolan

To the frontline combatants
in America's war on drugs.
God keep.

PROLOGUE

The worst part of a border crossing, Serafino Alvarez decided, was the act of getting up sufficient nerve to start. The desert was familiar, much the same on one side as the other, but at night it seemed a different place entirely, alien and hostile. You could step on rattlesnakes at night without warning, twist your ankle in a rat hole, stumble into cactus with the long, sharp thorns.

And, after nightfall, there were other dangers in the desert.

Alvarez wasn't a statistician—he could barely add or multiply, in fact, until it came to money—but he knew about the border's rate of violent crime. His bread and butter, not to mention his tequila, were dependent on his knowledge of such things.

At night the predators came out on both sides of the border, hot for easy pickings from the wets who made their way across in droves. The border scum knew well enough that every wetback headed for El Norte had some money squirreled away, perhaps a little jewelry, something in the nature of a family heirloom. Others came out strictly for the women, confident that an illegal alien wouldn't be quick to tell the police that she was raped while sneaking into the United States.

And there were others who enjoyed the sport of hunting men.

This evening Serafino Alvarez was more concerned about a different kind of predator. It had been thirteen days since he had rejected the demand for tribute from Sylvester Ramos, roughing up the big man's errand boy. Two weeks tomorrow, and he had been waiting every night for some reaction.

He had been drunk and feeling macho when the errand boy approached him with a hungry smile and the demand from Ramos. Alvarez was earning twenty dollars each for wets he led across the border, with a special discount rate for children. Ramos wanted half, paid off in weekly increments, to guarantee "protection."

Alvarez had laughed until the errand boy had gotten angry, slapping him and telling him to mind his manners. That was all it had taken for Alvarez to come out swinging with a bottle, following the first blow with fists and feet until the errand boy was curled up, sniveling, on the sawdust-covered floor of the cantina.

The next morning, after he sobered up, Alvarez had recognized his mistake, but it was too late to back down. He had his pride to think of, and he knew that Ramos would be fuming, anyway. Instead of half of Serafino's income, he would want two-thirds. He might not even take the money, preferring to make an example of Alvarez for his future "business partners."

Even so life went on. Alvarez had bills to pay, and an endless thirst for tequila. Thousands of his fellow countrymen were waiting for the chance to seek their fortunes in the north, and they needed a coyote with experience to get them there. If Alvarez stayed home at night, some other businessman would simply pocket all that cash.

Tonight's haul was fifteen wets. Three hundred dollars, less a discount for the boy who looked approximately nine or ten years old. Of course, the mother paid full price, plus seven dollars for her child.

He recognized a number of the wets from other trips across the border. Two or three of them had gone across last summer, maybe worked a while before the immigration service had scooped them up and sent them back to Mexico. A couple of the wets were regulars who made the journey every year, in time for harvest in the San Joaquin Valley, returning with their pockets filled to tide their families through another Baja winter. Others had been stopped in transit and returned before they ever had a chance to see the fabled streets of gold.

They all kept trying, and it wasn't Alvarez's job to tell them that the golden streets were merely asphalt, baking in the southern California sun. If some of them were swindled on their wages, crowded into miserable apartments barely fit for animals, so be it. Alvarez offered them a way across the borderline, and nothing more. It was a business, after all.

They crossed a half mile east of Tijuana, moving roughly parallel to Highway 805. It was seven miles to San Diego proper from their starting point, but Alvarez wasn't paid to take them all the way. From Otay Valley Road, around the halfway mark, his wets were on their own.

Assuming they ever got that far.

He concentrated on the trail, alert for signs of danger on the way. From time to time they crossed the tracks of other northbound wets, but that was standard. After sundown it was difficult to take a walk along the border strip without encountering other souls who were making their way across.

So far nothing suggested they were being followed, scouted for a raid. You never knew, of course, but so far things were looking good.

He checked the wets habitually to make sure they were keeping up, but it was dark out, no real moon to speak of, and he had Sylvester Ramos on his mind.

No wonder, then, that Alvarez failed to miss the boy.

HIS BLADDER FELT as if it would burst any moment, but he couldn't ask the group to wait. It was a simple thing to fall out of line and find himself a narrow gully where the tumbleweeds and cactus helped to screen him as he fumbled with the buttons of his fly. The rush of sweet relief, and in another moment he could catch up with the group. A couple of the men were still in sight, and he'd have to run only a little way.

The lights surprised him, blazing out of nowhere. Two in front at first, then another cutting off the group's retreat before they had a chance to run.

Surrounded.

Somehow they had passed the third man by and left him on their flank. A hulking shadow stood between the young boy and his mother now, two other shadows closing from the north.

He didn't understand the shouted orders, all in English, but he recognized the angry tone of voice and saw the weapons covering his mother and the rest. A sudden flash of panic almost made him run to her side, try to protect her, but a sense of self-preservation conquered the impulse and made him stand fast. Invisible, unnoticed by the men with guns, he stood and watched, recording every detail in his mind.

The men were Anglos. He could tell by the voices. Moments later, when their flashlight beams began to sweep across his mother and the rest, he picked out unfamiliar faces, memorizing each in turn.

A round face, with a bristling red mustache.

A long, thin face with downturned mouth and eyes like chips of slate.

An average face that did most of the talking, wire-rimmed glasses perched on the slightly crooked nose.

All three wore uniforms, but they weren't the forest green of the Border Patrol. Perhaps, he thought, the immigration people from the U.S.A. had a special squad these days.

The gringos made his mother and the rest line up, shoulder to shoulder, facing westward. The coyote, Alvarez, was speaking to the round-faced man in English, trying to negotiate with cash in hand. In Mexico, where institutionalized bribery—*la mordida,* the "little bite"—allowed policemen to survive on their pathetic salaries, the show of money almost always worked. But in the north . . .

Standing in the dark, he watched the money disappear as Round Face tucked it into his pocket. Alvarez appeared relieved at first until the Anglo shoved him back in line without another word. As if on cue, the flashlights all winked out, his mother and the rest transformed into a murky line of silhouettes.

The sudden gunfire shocked him, automatic weapons spitting jagged bolts of flame that lit the faces of his mother and the others. A scream rushed from his belly to his throat, but he contained it, both hands clasped across his mouth.

To make a sound or show himself meant instant death.

Despite the thunder in his ears, he heard the ugly sound of bullets striking flesh and bone, some of the human targets shouting as they died. The Anglos worked methodically, one gunner spraying left to right along the line, another working in reverse, while Round Face triggered short precision bursts at those who fell.

The hellish racket seemed to last forever, but in truth he knew that only seconds had elapsed before the guns fell silent. Standing fifty feet away, his nostrils crinkled at an acrid stench of fireworks that reminded him of celebrations in the village square.

No celebrations now.

The long-faced gringo switched his flashlight on and moved along the line of crumpled, twisted bodies. One by one he checked the faces, pausing here and there to prod a silent form before he moved along. The young boy saw his mother one last time, in profile, with her head thrown back, eyes closed in death.

He felt hot tears streaming down his cheeks, but he wouldn't allow himself to make a sound. If he were armed with a machine gun, like the gringos, then it might be different. He could make them pay.

Too late.

The men in uniform were leaving now, their flashlights bobbing through the sage and cactus, fading out of sight. He stood and waited several moments longer for the sound of a retreating vehicle.

The boy had a choice to make. He could continue northward, following the killers into San Diego, but he doubted whether he could make a living on his own.

Which left his second choice.

He couldn't help his mother now, and even though he understood the teachings of the church, believing she had gone on to a better place, he feared to touch her now. The dead weren't for handling unless you were a priest or undertaker, trained to deal with souls.

One choice.

He wiped a linen sleeve across his face to clean away the tears and dust. He stared at the huddled line of figures on the ground for a moment, then turned back in the direction of the border, retracing his steps in the darkness.

Alone.

1

Driving south toward Old Town on the San Diego Freeway, Johnny Gray switched on the radio and punched the preset button for an all-news station. There was trouble in the Middle East, as usual, and hurricanes forecast for the Caribbean. In Jacksonville a "pro-life" activist was facing trial on charges of conspiring to assassinate two surgeons at a neighborhood abortion clinic. The new mayor of Washington, D.C., was cracking down on drugs—again—and spokesmen for the DEA were optimistic that a recent seizure of cocaine in Florida had "hit the cartels where they live."

Good luck.

He saw the off ramp for Pacific Highway coming up and signaled for the lane change, falling into line behind a semi trailer hauling produce. He was early for the meet, and since his snitch had never once been punctual in eighteen months, he felt no need to push it.

Nice and easy all the way.

The local news came on, and Johnny turned the volume up a little. There had been gang-related violence in La Jolla, with a shooting that involved police. An embezzlement scandal was brewing in the city auditor's office. A group of upperclassmen at the city college had been nailed for cheating on their midterms.

Barely three days old, and they were already giving up on the massacre of fifteen Mexicans a few miles south of town. With one or two exceptions the dead had been identified, and relatives in Mexico were lining up to claim the bodies once the sheriff's office and the medical examiner were finished running tests. The solid information currently on file was thin enough to see through if you held it up against the light.

For starters the dead had clearly been illegal aliens, Mexican nationals crossing the border by night, which pushed them toward the bottom of everybody's priority list. They ranged in age from seventeen to forty-three, eleven men, four women, with three married couples in the batch. They'd been killed by close-range automatic fire, the crime scene littered with expended brass, and from the way their bodies had fallen, it looked as if they'd been mowed down execution-style. One of the victims, Serafino Alvarez, was a professional coyote, known on both sides of the border for his skill in moving wets across the line. A circling cloud of vultures had led two hikers to the murder site the morning after, and the rest was history.

Johnny Gray knew that much from the press, and because he maintained working contacts inside both the sheriff's department and the city police force. A storefront lawyer specializing in criminal cases and long-shot civil suits from nine to five, he needed all the contacts he could get.

They didn't hurt his after-hours business, either.

Gray's interest in the massacre was more than academic. Those who knew him by his old name—Bolan— would have understood at once why Johnny felt a need to check the case out on his own, involve himself in matters that were normally reserved for the authorities.

If anyone had asked him, Johnny might have answered that the need was in his blood, a living part of him that had sprung from private tragedy in childhood and taken root in the career his brother had pursued by fate or choice. Mack Bolan had been bucking impossible odds as long as Johnny could remember, first in Vietnam, then picking up the pieces of a shattered life and carrying the private war against his enemies. Along the way he had arranged for Johnny to be hidden—finally adopted—by another loving family, but military service in Grenada and a stint in law school weren't enough to satisfy the younger Bolan's craving for a challenge.

Challenge number one had been convincing his brother that he could use an ally in his lonely war. The elder Bolan's first reaction had been absolute rejection, a stubborn refusal to jeopardize his sole surviving kin. When it became apparent that Johnny meant to pursue his chosen course, with or without big brother's approval, they had reached a compromise of sorts. These days Johnny managed Strongbase One in San Diego, a secure communications relay link and safehouse on the coast.

The brothers had been through a lot together in the past few years, although Johnny played a relatively minor role in Bolan's war—campaigns in California, Arizona, Texas and a grueling run from coast to coast when they were called upon to baby-sit a federal witness marked for death. Between engagements Johnny kept his hand in on the local scene along the border, and he spoke with Bolan on average at least once a month by telephone. He never knew exactly what his brother was involved in one day to the next, but it was all the two of them could manage, allowing for security.

Pacific Highway carried him across the San Diego River, traffic slowing to a crawl beneath the Ocean Park

Freeway. He turned left on Taylor, circling Presidio Park into Old Town. The meet was set for half past ten, which left him fifteen minutes.

The massacre had captured Johnny's interest from the moment he had heard the news. It wasn't California's worst mass murder in recent memory—not even San Diego's worst—but it appeared to fall outside the normal run of psychopathic violence that normally monopolized the news. No sexual assault or robbery apparent from the evidence, no indication that a racist vigilante group had been involved. That left a mystery...or rather one of several Johnny Bolan-Gray had been collecting in the past few months.

The California-Baja border was a lawless, violent district at the best of times, but lately there had been an escalation in brutality that startled even veteran homicide investigators. There was nothing that would constitute a pattern yet, but soldier's intuition told him it was worth a closer look.

The snitch's name was Eddie Lopez. He'd dealt with Johnny in the past on several drug-related deals, and his information had always been reliable. It should have been, considering the fact that Eddie was a minor dealer in his own right, mostly grass, and he wasn't averse to giving up the competition when he had a chance.

There would be no snitches if it wasn't for self-interest, and Johnny knew the rules of the game. You paid for what you got and never expected too much from a simple business transaction. If the game went sour and you found out you were getting screwed, you settled the account by any means necessary.

Nothing ventured, nothing gained.

And what did he expect to gain from Eddie Lopez this time?

Insight possibly.

The tavern was a meeting place they had used before. It stood on neutral ground, away from Johnny's base in Pacific Beach and Eddie's game preserve in El Cajón. Even so there was a chance they might be spotted, but he'd take the chance.

Again.

They never went inside the bar to talk, considering the risks of being overheard. Sometimes they sat in Johnny's car, sometimes in Eddie's, and it worked out either way. Or had so far.

In every meet with a snitch on matters that pertained to sudden death there was a sense of danger. Johnny was accustomed to the feeling, and he always came prepared. The Smith & Wesson automatic slung beneath his arm was the new Model 4006, chambered in 10 mm, with a live round in the chamber and eleven in the magazine. Now standard issue for the FBI, with hot loads it combined the penetration of a Magnum with the knockdown power of an Army .45.

He parked outside the tavern, with a clear view of the street, and settled back to wait. It came as a surprise when he saw Eddie's Firebird rolling west along the boulevard at half past ten precisely. It was out of character to say the least, and Johnny scanned the next eight cars in line to check for tails.

So far so good.

His contact turned into the parking lot and found the empty slot beside him, facing in the opposite direction so the drivers' windows were aligned.

"Let's take a ride," Lopez suggested, beckoning.

"What's wrong with here?"

"We've got a lot to talk about," his snitch replied. "I don't like sitting still."

"Okay."

Johnny locked his car and took a walk around the Firebird, checking the empty space behind the driver's seat from force of habit. He was barely settled on the passenger side before Lopez wheeled out of the parking lot and back into traffic.

"You're looking nervous, Eddie."

"Fucking-ay."

"What's up?"

"You ask about some dead wets in the desert, sometimes you don't know where it'll lead you, dig?"

"Not yet."

"Let's say it wasn't just some offhand thing, all right?"

"I knew that off the top. You have some news for me, or what?"

"You want the news? Okay, let's try Sylvester Ramos."

"Say again?"

"You heard me right, man. Ramos called the shots on this one down the line."

"What's Ramos got to do with wetbacks, Eddie? Are you telling me that one of them was packing dope the sheriff's office didn't find?"

"No dope, man. Word I get, Sylvester's branching out. He wants to own the whole damn border, everything. He's running shit just like he always has, but now he's taxing everything that moves. Whatever comes across, including wets, the mover has to pay a toll."

"And this coyote didn't pay?"

"You'll have to draw your own conclusions, man. I didn't exactly have a lot of time for background research on the dear departed."

"I need more on Ramos, Eddie. If he's branching out, I have to get some details."

"Count me out, *compadre*. Playing with Sylvester ain't like baseball. He don't give you any strikes, you dig? First time you drop the ball, you're fucking out. Forever."

"What's the problem, Eddie? You're supposed to be the baddest dude in town."

"Don't yank my chain, okay? We both know Sylvester's in a different league. He drops a coin, I'm history. The same for you, man, if you get my drift."

"Somebody make you on this thing?"

"You shitting me?" But there was more concern in Eddie's tone than he was willing to admit. "I'm clean, all right? I want to keep it that way."

"Right."

"One thing you ought to know before you start to nose around."

"What's that?"

"The shooters on this deal, they weren't your usual."

"What's that supposed to mean?"

"It means they all wore bluesuits, dig it?"

"Cops?"

"You heard me right."

"If this is straight—"

"It's straight, okay?"

The chase car seemed to come from nowhere, sliding up beside them in the center lane and pulling just a yard or two ahead. No muzzle-flash in daylight, and the first hint Johnny had of danger came with the explosion of the windshield, pebbled safety glass all over everything as Eddie Lopez lost his face and lost control.

The Firebird swerved hard to the right and jumped the curb, momentum shearing off a mailbox and bringing them to rest against a concrete bus stop bench. Traveling without a seat belt, Johnny was propelled against the dashboard with force enough to knock the wind out of his lungs.

A second shotgun blast had punched holes in the driver's door as they were swerving, Eddie's dead hands slipping from the wheel. Almost miraculously Johnny found that he hadn't been hit. The blood that flecked his slacks and jacket had come from Lopez, splattered when the buckshot had taken out his face.

Johnny groped for the door handle, found it and spilled himself out onto the sidewalk. Thinking fast, he came up with the Smith & Wesson in his hand, prepared to return fire if the shooters were hanging around. He checked the street in both directions, found the traffic snarled and creeping, but the chase car had vanished.

A clean in-and-out.

The only question now: had they been tracking Eddie Lopez on an old beef, something totally divorced from Johnny's quest, or had Sylvester Ramos somehow learned of Johnny's interest in the desert massacre already?

More to the point, if Ramos *was* behind the shooting, who was the target?

He considered bugging out, and then decided it was too much trouble. If they checked the car for fingerprints, a hit from Johnny's military records would be guaranteed. He had a carry permit for the Smith, and it wouldn't take long to fabricate a cover story for his meet with Lopez. Something in the nature of a search for information, helping one of his assorted clients from the barrio. The rule of confidentiality would cover up his tracks quite nicely if he handled it correctly.

Settled, then.

He leaned against the Firebird, holstering his weapon, trying not to think of Eddie Lopez leaking in the driver's seat. He'd endure a short wait for the sirens, knowing what he had to do as soon as he was finished with his statement.

It was time to call the cavalry.

2

The Alabama gig had gone like clockwork, which was rare in Mack Bolan's line of work. He was accustomed to delays, obstructions, double crosses and snafus, but this time it had come together like a finely tuned machine.

Withdrawal was the easy part, all things considered. Driving south on Highway 10 from Mobile, he'd crossed the Mississippi line in forty minutes flat. He stopped at Escatawpa for a plate of barbecued ribs and used the pay phone for his mandatory after-action contact with the Stony Man exchange.

The telephone rang twice, four hundred miles away in Virginia's Blue Ridge Mountains, and an unfamiliar voice came on the line. He used the daily password that would tell his contact they were speaking on an open line, then waited while a scrambler was engaged. In spite of the precaution they would still restrict themselves to generalities or coded phrases, covering the one-in-a-million chance of a break in security.

"All ready, Striker. Go ahead, please."

There was no good reason, Bolan thought, why he should recognize the voice. He knew the major players intimately back at Stony Man Farm, but he wouldn't have recognized the second-stringers if they passed him on the street. In any case the operator wouldn't be on duty if he hadn't passed the screening process, rigorous enough to satisfy the FBI and CIA combined.

"I've solved that problem with the fisherman," Bolan said. "He's retired."

"No difficulties?"

"Nothing that I couldn't handle. Wonderland can have the small-fry if they're interested."

"We'll pass it on."

"That's it, then."

"Hold a second, Striker. We've got something for you from the coast."

An icy finger traced its way down Bolan's spine. "The coast" meant Johnny out in San Diego, and a contact on the Stony Man exchange would mean he didn't feel he could spare the time to leave a message in the normal way. There was an answering service in Los Angeles that handled Johnny's routine signals, passing word along to Bolan when he checked the board at rough biweekly intervals, but Stony Man was for emergencies.

"I'm listening."

"You're asked to get in touch ASAP."

"That's it?"

"Affirmative."

"When was it filed?"

"Noon yesterday."

"Received and understood."

He cradled the receiver, drawing several breaths and letting them escape while he took time to put his thoughts in order. It could still be anything, he told himself. There was no reason for alarm.

Not yet.

But he couldn't help thinking of the time when Johnny was a kid in Massachusetts and a careless word had blown his cover at a private school. The Mafia was quick to strike, and Bolan had spilled a sea of blood to get his brother back again intact.

Forget it!

Anything like that, and there was no way Johnny could have called it in. No way would he have jeopardized security by letting any adversary know the number of the Stony Man exchange.

A crisis, then, but not the kind that meant you had to move right now, this minute, or your world would fall apart. He still had time to think while he went looking for another telephone.

Security at Stony Man was excellent, but Bolan based his day-to-day survival on the fact that he took nothing for granted. The odds against an interception on his call were astronomical, and getting it unscrambled would require a miracle of sorts, but he'd find another telephone before he made his second call. It couldn't hurt, and he was only talking minutes in the greater scheme of things. If Johnny needed him right now, this instant, they were both out of luck.

Noon yesterday. Twenty-five hours and change since his brother had left the message. Bolan knew it could be a lifetime, but he wouldn't let his own imagination do him in. Chill out and make the call as soon as possible, find out what Johnny had to say.

He drove to Moss Point, six or seven miles through piny woods, before he found another public telephone. The operator quoted an amount, and Bolan dropped coins into the slot.

The number he dialed in San Diego was a cutout relay, switching automatically to yet another line before the third ring sounded in his ear. If anybody took the time to trace the call, they'd be looking at a rented room in West Covina near Los Angeles, and they'd watch in vain. As long as the equipment functioned and the rent was paid on time by money orders through the mail, no one set foot inside the place.

The third ring shunted Bolan's call to Strongbase One, and Johnny picked up two rings later, sounding tired but otherwise all right.

"I got the message," Bolan told his brother. "This line's not secure."

"No problem. Have you got some time?"

"To talk?"

"To visit."

Bolan frowned. It wasn't often that his brother called for help.

"I might."

"It could get hairy."

"I'll bring scissors."

Johnny chuckled on the other end, a weary sound. "That wouldn't be a bad idea."

"What kind of deadline are we on?"

"Unknown. I had a close shave yesterday, but I'm not sure the barber's satisfied."

"Okay," Bolan said, calculating times. "I'll be there, hopefully sometime tonight. I'll have to call you from the airport."

"Fair enough. I'll be here."

"Watch yourself, all right?"

"I always do."

The line went dead, and Bolan spent a moment staring at the silent telephone before he backtracked to his car. The "close shave" reference had to mean a near-miss kill attempt, but that was all he could gather on the land line. Going into detail from a distance would be risky, not to mention time-consuming. At the moment he was more interested in traveling at speed than standing in a Mississippi phone booth, hearing Johnny's problems from a thousand miles away.

Bolan knew all about losing family from personal experience. The violent deaths of his parents and sister had launched his one-man war against the savages, and it had been a damn close call for Johnny that time. He had long since stopped counting all the friends and loved ones sacrificed along the way.

But not this time.

Not if the Executioner had anything to say about the outcome.

Jackson, Mississippi, coming up.

The warrior found that he could hardly wait.

THE CALL FROM MACK HELPED Johnny to relax a little, even though his thoughts were still in overdrive. He didn't grieve for Eddie Lopez as an individual, drug dealer that he was, but there was something in a narrow brush with death that left your nerves on edge, stretched thin and as tight as a piano wire for hours afterward. Sometimes for days. He found the agitation helped him think, if he could only exercise the necessary discipline to hold the more bizarre imaginings in check.

His interview with the police had been prolonged and quasi-hostile once he started quoting the attorney-client privilege line. It was a safety hatch that spared him even naming the anonymous—and nonexistent—client, and it served him well, but San Diego homicide investigators weren't known for bowing graciously to local protocol.

For a start, the local force had problems: one of the lowest homicide solution rates in California, possibly in the United States; endemic violence linked directly to the border, drugs, illegal aliens and gangs; pervasive accusations of abuse directed toward minorities that sapped police morale each time an officer was disciplined, suspended or discharged. There hadn't been a major riot yet, although Johnny sometimes wondered why. In many ways the San Diego atmosphere was parallel to that found in Miami, where a Latin culture clashed with old-line Anglo values, and the war was definitely not confined to words.

His problem at the moment was twofold. First, he had to backtrack Eddie Lopez, try to scope out who would want him dead and why. If there was any link at all between the desert massacre and Eddie's death, the near-miss Johnny had survived, he had to know about it soon before the shooters made a try at picking up their spare.

And second, he was more concerned than ever with the loss of fifteen lives two nights earlier. The mention of Sylvester Ramos as a moving force behind the massacre had only made it more imperative that evidence be gathered, a solution found.

But not, he now suspected, in a court of law.

If the killers had been "bluesuits," as alleged by Lopez, there would be a problem dealing with police. It didn't mean the whole department was corrupt, by any means, but he'd have to pick and choose before he risked a contact, weighing the risks beforehand, watching out for a double cross. It wouldn't be the first time that a payoff led to homicide, and he'd have to watch his back from this point on.

One major question was how had Eddie Lopez known—or come to think—the triggermen had been police? No matter how he turned the problem inside out or stood it on its head, his options were the same. First, it might have been a lie, concocted by Lopez or some unknown third party. Second, and highly improbable, the killers might be boasting of their crime.

And third, there could be a surviving witness to the massacre.

At first glance that seemed unlikely, but stranger things had happened. In the desert darkness and confusion it was possible the firing squad had overlooked somebody, letting him or her escape to tell the tale. Except that sharing that report would be a risky proposition, approaching suicide.

He had debated with himself before he placed the call to Stony Man. Requesting help was one thing—Johnny knew he needed it on this one—but requesting help from brother Mack was something else. It wasn't just the macho thing, a younger brother's need to prove himself a man; they were effectively beyond all that. One problem was his brother's schedule, crowded as it was, with Johnny always in the dark about his moves before the fact of an engagement with the enemy. For all he knew, Mack might be booked for weeks or months ahead, with no time to spare for mixing in a border war.

Another problem was his brother's strict refusal to go one-on-one in violent confrontations with police.

To Mack Bolan the men in blue were always "soldiers of the same side," no matter how they soiled their badges and themselves by fraternizing with the enemy. The dirty cops weren't immune to Bolan's wrath, by any means, but he had always managed to avoid a killing confrontation with the law.

And that, Johnny thought, could become a major difficulty if Sylvester Ramos was behind the desert massacre, assuming that his triggermen were actually police.

He didn't like the thought of Mack approaching San Diego with his options limited, compelled to fight with one hand tied behind his back. The enemy would recognize no such restrictions.

But, in any case, he had made the call.

There had been nowhere else to turn.

His mind recalled the times when Mack had literally saved his life, with some occasions when the shoe was on the other foot. The last thing Mack had ever wanted for his brother was a life of everlasting war, the very life he had selected for himself, but he had finally accepted Johnny's choice without recriminations.

Maybe it was something in the blood line, Johnny thought. Their father was an immigrant who had gone to fight the Nazis in another war. Mack had found his enemy in Vietnam at first and later on the home front where a savage breed of predator was threatening the nation's life and honor. Johnny had been proud to serve his country in Grenada and the Middle East, but discharge from military service hadn't meant an end to war. He recognized the enemies around him, trained to spot them by a lifetime of experience, and he couldn't stand by inactive while the savages proceeded to defile his home.

The legal work was part of it, of course. Injustice wasn't limited to terrorist assassinations or the violence meted out by gangs to hapless citizens. It happened every day, in every walk of life, and Johnny's day job was a way of helping out the poor and the powerless when they were being stepped on by the System. Jousting in the courtroom had its own rewards, but he had grown up as a fighter, and the plain truth was that Johnny sometimes missed the rush that came with swift, decisive action.

Not that he was hooked on violent death; far from it. He had killed his first man in Grenada, others since, and while he didn't brood about the fact, he recognized the scars on his soul. Sometimes a man not only had the right to kill, he had a concrete duty to oppose the savages by any means at his disposal, to prevent atrocities and stop the predators from gobbling up a few more innocents.

This time, for instance, when the stakes were sixteen dead and counting.

He had work to do before he started waiting for his brother's call. If there was a surviving witness to the recent massacre, he had to make an effort at discovery. It might not lead to anything the D.A.'s office would approve, but he wasn't concerned about the legal rules of evidence on this one.

Before the smoke cleared Ramos and his syndicate might have to settle out of court.

3

Bolan woke on the approach to San Diego International, the chimes of an obligatory seat belt warning interrupting murky dreams. He had no concrete memory of what he had dreamed, and had no faith in psychic precognition to begin with, but a nagging sense of apprehension lingered as he pressed the armrest button and returned his seat to its original upright position.

Jackson's airport had slowed him down, with a six-hour wait before the next flight out to San Diego, but he had no choice. On top of the delay there was an hour's stop in Texas to contend with, but he swallowed the anxiety and summoned up the inbred patience that had served him well on countless all-night watches in the past.

One bonus was the relaxation of security since Operation Desert Storm had been successfully resolved. He trusted his Beretta 93-R and its shoulder rigging to the check-through luggage, ready with a bogus piece of FBI identification if anybody raised a beef about the gun.

No sweat.

If they were scanning check-through bags, it was a joke. As far as more elaborate hardware was concerned, he knew that Johnny had connections on the coast, along with a substantial stockpile ready at his fingertips.

The 727 circled over San Diego Bay and doubled back to catch the eastbound runway. Studying the lights of San

Diego spread below him, Bolan called up mental images of yet another visit in the early days of his campaign against the Mafia. His San Diego siege had been successfully resolved, but not without a price.

Too many memories.

Sometimes it seemed that there was nowhere he could go on earth without encountering a swarm of ghosts—some friendly, some distinctly hostile. None of them could touch him, but they followed Bolan everywhere, relentless in attendance at his every move.

It was the price of taking up a soldier's life-style, coping with the dead that way. They didn't trouble Bolan in the sense of preying on his conscience, although the friendly dead sometimes recalled occasions when he could have done a little something different, something extra, to protect a friend. A soldier lived with that, avoiding self-reproach, incorporating valid criticism in his mind-set, covering his bets for next time, and the conflict after that.

He waited, staring out the window as they taxied slowly toward the terminal. Around him restless passengers were on their feet and digging into overhead compartments, flight attendants forced to urge them back into their seats, all plastic smiles in spite of the annoyance they had to feel. No rush, as far as Bolan was concerned. He'd be on the ground soon, moving through the terminal, and Johnny would be waiting for him.

They'd had no contact since their conversation on the telephone that morning, and he knew that anything could happen in the space of half a day.

He blanked the mental images, refusing to consider all the different ways a man could die in thirteen hours. Johnny knew the game by heart, and he would take no unnecessary risks. On the other hand, some risks were absolutely necessary. Unavoidable, in fact.

He picked his brother out three steps beyond the gate, a ready smile and solid handshake as they greeted each other after—what?—three months apart. No conspicuous display of emotion in the public eye. They might as easily have been two businessmen keeping a routine appointment.

"Looking good," Johnny said.

"You the same," his brother replied, and meant it.

"Luggage?"

"One bag coming through."

"The carousels are this way."

Johnny led him through the concourse, moderately crowded at this time of night, until they reached the baggage claim area. Several passengers from Bolan's flight were there ahead of them. They waited, holding conversation to a minimum, until the flashing lights came on and the conveyer belt began to move, disgorging luggage from the Jackson-Dallas run.

"That's it."

He snared his bag on the first pass, noting there was no sign of tampering with the locks. A few moments later they cleared the terminal, Johnny steering the course to an adjacent parking garage, where his Buick was parked on level three. A cautious walk-around and scan for watchers turned up nothing. Johnny paid three dollars at the exit gate, and then they were rolling east on Harbor Drive to catch Pacific Highway northbound.

"So let's have it," Bolan said when they were under way.

"Two nights before I made the call to Stony Man some wets and their coyote walked into an ambush a few miles south of town. Fifteen dead. You might have heard some mention of it on the news."

"I did."

"We're getting used to violence on the border, but the numbers were still a standout. The shooters all used automatic weapons, with the victims lined up execution-style. No rape or robbery. I started checking into it."

"On whose behalf?"

"My own. It has a smell about it. Anyway, I asked around, made contact with some people who keep an eye on the border... professionally."

"Okay."

"I made connections with a snitch named Eddie Lopez. Small-time dealer, ratted on the competition any time he got the chance, that kind of thing. We took a ride, and he was running down some information on the shootings when we caught a broadside from a chase car. Lopez bought it."

"Any follow-up?" Bolan asked.

"The police, of course. I shined them on with the attorney-client privilege line. No comeback on the shooters yet. If they were after me, they haven't made another try."

"Would that be luck or planning?"

"Either way I'm in the clear unless they had some kind of line on Eddie's contacts going in."

"I wouldn't rule it out."

"I'm not."

"You mentioned information," Bolan prompted.

"That's right. He blamed the killings on a local dealer named Sylvester Ramos. Big-time all the way on that one. He's been heavy into drugs the past few years, expanding into other forms of contraband if Lopez was correct."

"The human kind?"

"From what I got he isn't moving wets himself. It's more a shot at dominating border traffic down the line, protection payoffs from the other smugglers, the coyotes, this and that. Along the way he steps on any competition where it hurts."

"You're figuring the massacre as an example?"

"That's what Lopez thought. I don't have anything to contradict him yet."

"I'd like to hear some more about this Ramos character."

"I thought you might. Age thirty-four, five-nine, black hair, brown eyes. I've got some mug shots at the house courtesy of LAPD. He was born in Los Angeles, precise date uncertain. He claims the Fourth of July as his birthday, and no one's been able to prove otherwise. His parents were waiting on naturalization when Sylvester came along, so he's covered on citizenship."

"Rap sheet?" Bolan asked.

"A beauty, starting at the age of twelve."

"I thought the juvey records were destroyed at age eighteen."

"We have our ways," Johnny said. "Sylvester's been hauled in for damn near everything you can imagine. Grand theft auto was his favorite till he discovered drugs, but he's got counts of B and E, concealed weapons, rape, attempted rape, three or four kinds of assault, with and without deadly weapons. You name it."

"All juvenile?"

"You got it. As an adult, he's done time for GTA and possession of cocaine, back before the 'war on drugs' got hot. Two arrests for attempted murder in 1981 and '83, both dismissed when the complaining victims changed their minds and refused to testify. By that time he was running with the in-crowd on coke and grass, relocated in San Diego and bringing loads over the border on a regular basis. On the downside he's never been popped with a shipment, and three informants have died in the past two years, trying to help the D.A. make a case that would stand up in court."

"I take it he runs the operation now."

"Since '87," Johnny replied. "His boss, one Hector Gomez, bought it in a local restaurant that April. Sitting by the window like an idiot when someone comes along and strafes him with an AK-47. Investigators can't decide if it was Ramos cleaning house, or maybe someone from a rival gang who got cold feet and split without a follow-up."

"What kind of competition is he facing?" Bolan asked.

"The border makes it rough to calculate offhand. Everybody and his cousin tries to run shit through Tijuana one time or another. It's like Matamoros or Nuevo Laredo that way. Heavy year-round tourist traffic, servicemen, a ton of college kids. You name it."

"Syndicates?"

"That's different. This side of the border he's been feuding with the Escalante brothers—Julio, Rico and Guillermo. You can scratch Guillermo off the list, though. Someone wired his hot tub with explosives two weeks back and took him out. Julio and Rico have been lying low since then, but they're around here somewhere."

"How does their operation compare with Sylvester's in volume?"

"About one-third the size, if we can trust the federal estimates of what gets through the net. Last count they had about three dozen soldiers, but it's safe to bet that Ramos has removed a few since then."

"Across the border?"

"Two main families control the traffic in and out of Baja. Both grease the *federales* to keep product moving out of Tijuana on a regular basis. The Aguelo family, run by daddy Julio and sons, is probably the dominant concern in terms of cash and hardware, but the second runner-up isn't hurting. That would be the Cortez family, brothers Angel and Jésus, with six or seven cousins playing second-string."

"Angel and Jésus?"

Johnny shrugged. "I guess their parents were religious. Anyway, it didn't take. The Cortez family runs a cat food factory outside of Ensenada, with their product sold in stores all over Mexico. The rumor is, some of their competition feeds the kitty now and then."

"Hard feelings with the Ramos operation?"

"Nothing on the surface. The DEA says Ramos buys from both families, taking advantage of their Colombian connections. Apparently he's concentrating his efforts on this side of the border, trying to nail down anything that moves across the line. We don't have anything in the way of documented complaints from smalltimers, but word is he's muscled at least a dozen independents out of business in the past twelve months. Buried about the same number, give or take."

"A prince."

"The cream."

"I'd say it's time somebody skimmed the pot."

"You have a plan in mind?"

"I'm working on it. Can you tell me any more about the massacre?"

"I've got a list of names at home," Johnny said. "Fourteen wets and their coyote, if it does us any good. One thing, though..."

"Go ahead."

"Before he bought it Lopez told me the triggermen were cops."

"You buy it?"

Johnny shrugged. "I haven't got enough to go on yet. Thing is, if he's correct, he had to hear it somehow, right? I mean, he either got it through the grapevine, from one of the shooters talking, or there must be someone else."

"A witness," Bolan suggested.

"I'm hoping."

"Even so it won't be easy running down."

"I know. About the cops..."

"The maybe cops," the warrior said. "Let's cross that one when we get there. I'm still thinking Ramos at the moment."

"Right."

"The guys who want it all like peace and quiet. Ramos has been stepping on the opposition where he can, and so far no one's doing much about it, right?"

"Including the police."

"So maybe what he needs to shake him up is a response he can't ignore. Resistance on his own home turf, and maybe on the other side."

"It's worth a try."

"What kind of hardware do you have on hand?"

"A fair assortment. If it's not in stock, I've got reliable connections who can fill the gaps."

"I'll need more information on the man," Bolan told his brother.

"Done. I've got his home address and phone number, his leading girlfriend's, two or three main spots where he transacts his business, afternoons and evenings. It's been plotted on a city map, along with home addresses for his top lieutenants. Mugs and background files on them, as well.''

''That ought to get me started.''

''Hey, there's more. I ran a check through Wonderland and got a call back just as I was leaving for the airport.''

''Hal?''

''The next best thing.''

The thought of Leo Turrin brought a smile to Bolan's lips. They had been adversaries once, and friends for longer than he cared to think about. From working as a federal mole inside the Mafia Turrin had moved on to a desk at Justice, where he still chafed for the action of the ''old days'' he had left behind.

''What's up with Washington?''

''Some interesting news. They tapped a vein at the DEA and came up with some source material. Ramos is supposed to have a cutting plant somewhere in El Cajón. I've got a couple of snitches we can lean on for an address if you're interested.''

''I'm interested,'' Bolan replied. ''But I'll do the leaning by myself. No point in burning any bridges you don't have to.''

''Right.'' Reluctantly his brother saw the sense in that. ''Okay. The other word was on a shipment due sometime tomorrow or the next day. Nothing that would pin it down, but we can work on that from this end.''

''That and the address list ought to get us started, anyway. About that witness...''

''I've been thinking,'' Johnny told him. ''If the sheriff's office hasn't heard the rumbles, they'd be interested. There might be some way to finesse a deal.''

"And if your snitch was right about the shooters being cops, they run a fifty-fifty chance of being county."

"So I play it nice and easy. Say I've been retained by one or more survivors of the victims, with an eye toward civil suits. I'm checking out a rumor on surviving witnesses. I should get something just from their reactions to the notion. If they're on it, maybe I can hitch a ride. If not, the hint may get them rolling. We could use a few more eyes."

"That pretty much depends on who they're really working for," Bolan said.

"If they're dirty, they'll be looking that much harder. Sylvester might not care about a witness—hell, he might enjoy it, having someone spread the word—but cops won't like the thought of someone out there who can finger them as triggers for the family."

"Did anybody ever tell you you were devious?"

"I take it as a compliment," Johnny answered, smiling.

They were rolling west on Garnet, picking up Soledad Mountain Road for the winding run north to La Jolla. It was the fourth time Bolan had approached his brother's home this way, and there was something different to be noticed every time. Some new construction here and there, sporadic roadwork, all the trivia of daily life in progress. It reminded Bolan of the world he had given up in preference for a warrior's lonely road, but he wouldn't have changed the past.

Correction.

For perhaps the hundred thousandth time he thought it could have made a difference at the very start if he had been home to help his father with the Pittsfield loan sharks who had made his final days a living hell. Per-

haps, if Mack had been around to take the pressure off
and—

No.

To really make a difference intervention would have
been required before his father had logged those debts.
That would have meant a steady paying job at home, no
Army, no time spent in Vietnam. And if the sharks had
come regardless, if his father's stubborn pride had rejected help from family, there would have been no Executioner to take them out.

So much for changing history.

The weariness crept up behind him like a sneak thief,
tugging at his eyelids now. His in-flight nap had failed to
compensate for three days on the firing line without relief. When they were safely tucked away inside Strongbase, he'd check out Johnny's files, perhaps enjoy a meal
and get some sleep.

The San Diego blitz would start with Bolan fresh and
fit.

At dawn.

4

Luis Calvada was the first name on his list as Bolan motored north on Fletcher Parkway into El Cajón. The first gray light of dawn was leeching shadows from the streets around him, driving back the night. He navigated from the map that Johnny had prepared, with key locations marked in red, approaches and escape routes traced in green. A gym bag on the floor behind the driver's seat held Bolan's choice of field equipment for the morning's action, a variety of hardware that should see him through at least the first part of the day.

He'd decided not to go with Ramos off the top. It could have been a relatively simple thing to strike at the dealer, maybe end the war in one fell swoop. But there was more involved than simply rubbing out a local cocaine baron. If he meant to learn the truth about the massacre that had preceded Johnny's call, he had to give the game some time. Apply the necessary pressure, right, but dig for facts along the way.

Eliminating Ramos off the mark would throw his network into chaos and effectively destroy their chance of finding out who gave the order for the desert slaughter. And without that information they could never hope to tag the triggermen.

A more oblique approach, then, starting near the top and sending shock waves out in all directions.

The reports in hand identified Luis Calvada as number three in the Sylvester Ramos family, charged with the coordination of deliveries from the south. He also handled most of the enforcement problems locally, suppressing opposition when the need arose.

And on the side he was a legendary party animal, renowned for keeping women in reserve and staying up all night, most nights, to celebrate whatever came to mind.

Calvada's party house was located on Hacienda Drive. Bolan had no trouble with a parking space at 6:30 a.m., leaving his car next door to the target. He locked the driver's door and opened up the back, leaning in to retrieve a silenced Ingram MAC-10 from the gym bags and stuff extra magazines into his pockets. Then he cut across the lawn, bypassing the front door in favor of a flanking move.

He found a lookout snoozing on the patio beside the pool, his jacket hanging open to reveal a stainless-steel automatic in a shoulder harness. Bolan tapped the man on his forehead with the silencer, then was forced to repeat the move before the sleepy eyes opened and swam into focus. As the brain kicked in, instant panic registered on the man's face.

"Calvada?" the Executioner demanded. Bolan knew the answer, but wanted to verify it. The sentry's eyes flicked sharply toward the house behind him. "Where?" the warrior pressed.

"Hey, man—"

"One chance."

"Upstairs. First bedroom on the left."

"Sleep tight." He rapped the sentry on the temple with the butt of the Ingram.

Bolan found the sliding doors on the patio unlocked and made his way inside. He took the stairs three at a time, clearing the second-floor landing in four long strides. The first door on his left was closed, but Bolan tried the knob and found it wasn't locked.

It was dark inside the bedroom, but he found a light switch and flicked it on. Three pairs of feet protruded from the rumpled sheets and blankets at the bottom of a king-size bed. Two were female, according to their size and delicacy, with a pair of size elevens sandwiched in between.

He caught a handful of bedding, whipped it clear and exposed tangled bodies on the mattress. The redhead on the right was the first to awaken, and no modesty was involved as she rolled onto her back, checking out Bolan's face and the weapon he carried. "Oh, shit," she whispered.

"Take a hike," Bolan growled.

"You mean it?"

"It's a one-time offer."

"Hey, I'm out of here."

She scooped up her clothes on the move and disappeared. It crossed his mind that she might call for reinforcements, but Calvada had begun to stir. The brunette on his left still lay comatose, one arm flung across the mobster's waist.

"Hey!"

"This is your life, Calvada. What's left of it, anyway."

"Who the fuck are you?"

"Your nightmares come to life."

"So what do you want, man?"

"Information, for a start."

"I ain't no fucking snitch."

"So die."

The Ingram found a point above Calvada's nose and locked there, Bolan's finger tightening around the trigger.

"Jesus, wait!"

"For what?"

"You want to talk, what say I get some clothes on first?"

"No time for fashion statements."

"Shit."

"Your choice."

"Okay, man, run it down."

"Four nights ago, due south of town. A shooting. Fifteen people bought it."

"Sure, I watch the news."

"I want to know who Ramos used."

"You kidding me? That's wetbacks, man. That's shit."

There was a flicker in the man's eyes that sabotaged his outraged posture of veracity. No sale.

"I guess that's all we've got to talk about." The Ingram rose once again.

"Well, shit, I could be wrong."

"Oh, yeah?"

"It happens. Wets, you said?"

"*You* said."

"Yeah, right. It could be someone's stepping on Sylvester's toes, you know? Intruding on his territory, like."

"I'm listening."

"I really hate this, man. If I could have my fucking robe..."

It lay across a chair, perhaps a pace from the bedside.

"Go."

"Hey, thanks, man. You're all right."

Calvada made the move, the brunette barely stirring as he pushed her arm aside and rolled across the mattress, sitting up. Instead of reaching for the robe, though, Bolan's pigeon made a swift grab for the nightstand, whipping the drawer open and shoving his right hand inside.

Too late.

The Ingram stuttered, Parabellum manglers raking Calvada's flank and dumping him onto the carpet in a lifeless tangle of arms and legs. The brunette muttered something in her sleep and languidly rolled over.

The Executioner was out of time. He left the woman sleeping, with Calvada crumpled on the floor. No opposition waited for him as he left that house of death the way he came.

Bolan had gotten a near-admission from the pistolero, anyway, before he had died. Better than nothing to start with.

But he still had miles to go before he reached the finish line.

ARMANDO RIVAS never really liked the morning shift, but he wasn't in a position to complain when they had shipments coming in. The more shit he could process through the cutting plant, the more cash he took home. It was a simple rule of thumb, and getting up at six o'clock a couple of times a month was no great price to pay for what he earned each week.

He had to give Sylvester credit for his scheduling, the way he staggered shipments day and night. There was no schedule you could count on, and they were always changing routes to fox the DEA and local narcs. It might not qualify as genius, but the job got done, and their losses were kept in the five to eight percentile range each year. Miami's syndicates were happy if they only gave up ten, fifteen percent en route to the consumer.

Whatever else you said about Sylvester Ramos, you could never fault him on his brains.

This morning Rivas was the first to show up at the house on Palomar in southern El Cajón. He liked to be there, waiting, when his crew came in. It let them know he was on the job, no dipshit they could take advantage of by slacking off or slipping just a little something extra into their pockets from the cutting table.

He'd caught a lab rat stealing once, and that was all it had taken. They'd taken him to the basement, lately soundproofed so the neighbors couldn't hear, and spent two hours teaching him the error of his ways.

Before they shot him.

The other lab rats were made to stand and watch the whole thing. That afternoon, when it was time to break for lunch, none of them had seemed to have their usual appetite, and that was fine. Rivas's papa had taught him that a lesson ought to hurt. That way you knew the students would remember for a while.

The cutting plant was camouflaged as residential property, surrounded by the homes of working families who didn't have the faintest idea what was going on next door. There was a junior high school two blocks over, and it tickled Rivas sometimes, thinking that the coke they stepped on here would make its way all over town before it wound up in some teenybopper's snotty nose a short walk from the place where it began.

It didn't bother Rivas, knowing that a portion of the shit he helped adulterate and package would be sold to children. It would also go to movie stars in Hollywood, musicians on the Sunset Strip and God knows who throughout southern California. With the volume they were doing now Sylvester had a shot at reaching San Francisco in a year or so.

The big time.

Rivas had been waiting for the gravy train his whole life, and now that he'd dragged himself on board, he wouldn't let a trivial encumbrance like a conscience slow him down. Surviving in the barrio, you burned out early on the golden rule and learned that looking out for number one was all that really mattered in the world. If someone helped you out, then you rewarded them with loyalty while it lasted...or until a better offer came along.

And if someone tried to fuck you over, you got even. All the way.

This morning Rivas checked in the lab rats and staked out his gunners. Three men to watch the cutting plant was standard, all of them inside to keep from tipping off the neighbors. There had been no problems during the eighteen months they'd been using the facility, but every day was new. The world was full of jackals looking for a freebie, and a man who lacked the strength or courage to defend himself was no real man at all.

Rivas didn't really watch the lab rats, being an executive and all. One of his shooters handled the surveillance, letting the boss kick back in a separate room—his "office"—and enjoy the pornographic magazines he brought to work each day. He wasn't what you'd call a reader, but the text was bullshit, anyway: "Amanda is a premed student with a minor in philosophy. She works with homeless orphans on semester breaks and loves to knit when she is not involved in college sports."

Yeah, right.

The explosion almost knocked Rivas from his chair. He tossed the magazine aside and bolted for the door, an automatic pistol leaping to his hand. The first thing he thought of was an accident, some kind of fuck-up in the lab, but then it struck him that they weren't cooking anything, just cutting coke, repackaging the shit when it was stepped on half a dozen times. They didn't have a Bunsen burner in the house.

The gunfire made his mind up for him, automatic weapons chattering, the softer sound of bullets striking wood and plaster. Someone screamed, a painful sound, with fear and anger mixed up together, which was cut off sharply by another burst of fire.

He hesitated in the open doorway, smelling dust and cordite, knowing it was his job to repel invaders from the cutting plant. Sylvester trusted him and paid him well for this one thing.

He moved along the corridor, a few strides toward the lab through swirling dust and smoke. A human figure lurched in front of him, unsteady on his feet, and when he turned to face him, Rivas recognized one of the lab rats, fresh blood streaming down his face from where a fist-size portion of his scalp was sheared away. A sub-machine gun rattled in the midst of chaos, and the lab rat toppled forward onto his bloody face.

Rivas found himself a piece of wall and flattened against it, knowing stucco was a poor shield against determined automatic fire. The first burst might not take him, but he couldn't hold his place for long if he came under fire. Retreating made a lot of sense—the back door waiting for him, with an easy run across the yard and hop the neighbor's decorative wooden fence—but that was running, and he couldn't let it go at that.

He had a job to do, and never mind that he could see the cutting plant was trashed already, with the shipment blown away. Some of it maybe getting into his eyes and nostrils now, because he felt a little funny, as if his energy were coming back in overdrive.

All right.

So, if he couldn't save the place, at least he had a shot at payback, let the sneaking bastards know they were in a fight. And if they dropped him, it was still the macho thing to do.

He took another snort of the polluted air and lurched back to his feet, the automatic cocked and braced in both hands as he braced himself to make the move. In front of him another figure loomed out of the mist, and Rivas knew it had to be the enemy—a big guy, packing a machine gun, with a pair of plastic goggles and a surgical mask concealing his identity.

Rivas bellowed a battle cry and squeezed off two hasty rounds that missed his target by at least a yard. No matter. In a few more seconds he could press his piece against the bastard's chest and guarantee a kill shot.

Except he didn't have a few more seconds as the submachine gun opened up and cut him off below the knees. He fell across the line of fire, a solid hammer stroke against his ribs, the impact flipping Rivas over onto his back.

All done.

Rivas understood that he was dying, but it didn't hurt. Not yet. The coke perhaps. He took another ragged breath to cut the pain and closed his eyes.

THE CLUB ON ALVARADO in La Mesa was a favorite of Sylvester Ramos and his cronies, drawing them at least two nights a week. It featured decent food, overpriced drinks and waitresses whose skimpy costumes stopped a hair this side of making it a topless bar. The private rooms in back were good for all-night poker games or conferences on business matters that required a bit more peace and quiet.

It wasn't just that Ramos liked the club, however. Ramos owned it, through an "understanding" with the two proprietors of record. They cut Ramos in for fifty-one percent, and he allowed the club to stand and wives and families to go on breathing San Diego smog without a sudden, violent interruption of their lives.

It was the oldest racket in the world, and it was still effective.

Somehow Johnny had acquired a floor plan of the club. When asked about it, he had only smiled and shrugged, not interested in spelling out the details.

Fair enough.

With what he had the Executioner was ready to deliver a surprise for Ramos, one more in the series of surprises that had marked the morning. Shock waves should be rippling through the Ramos camp by now, but the reports would still be vague, confused, no angle for the dealer to pursue in terms of payback.

Bolan meant to give him targets as the day went on, but it was early yet. No point in rushing things and spoiling the suspense.

The club wouldn't be open until noon, three hours yet, but there were two cars in the parking lot when Bolan nosed his rental in and found himself a slot in back. The kitchen crew, no doubt, but they could still be armed. He took no chances going in, the satchel slung across one shoulder, the Beretta filling his hand.

The back door wasn't locked, and Bolan slipped inside without alerting either of the young men who were making preparations for another busy day and night.

One of them had the big refrigerator open, taking stock of their supplies, his partner kneeling and doing something with the grill.

"We're closing for repairs," Bolan said, watching both men jump.

They turned to him, eyes gone wide, a swift glance back and forth before the older of the two beside the grill reached for a gleaming butcher knife. A better look at the Beretta froze him with his hand outstretched, still empty.

"Think again," the Executioner suggested. "If you're smart, you'll know it's time to leave."

They took the hint, and Bolan watched them from the doorway long enough to see their cars burn rubber in the parking lot. It didn't matter if they raced to find a telephone. He needed only seconds now, and he was finished.

Bolan placed his satchel on the floor and toed it underneath the grill. There would be gas lines running underneath, and that would help. He checked the main room briefly, calling out to verify that he hadn't missed any members of the crew, then backtracked to his car.

All set.

The remote control detonator was no larger than a pack of cigarettes. He fired up the rental, pulled toward the exit from the parking lot and hesitated for another heartbeat as he keyed the switch. Behind him walls and insulation muffled the initial blast, but then the gas lines blew and rolling flames exploded from the shattered walls and roof. A piece of cowling from the air conditioner crashed down beside him, and he stood on the accelerator, rolling east, with dark smoke filling his rearview mirror.

Three for three, and he was on a roll. Beside him on the seat was a list of targets with the first three scribbled out, a full page yet to go.

But first he had to make a call.

5

The directory in the courthouse lobby steered Johnny to the fourth-floor sheriff's office, and he followed posted signs from there to Homicide. He had called ahead for an appointment with Sergeant Escobar, in charge of the county's ongoing mass-murder investigation. He turned up, expecting a crusty old veteran, and met his first surprise of the day as the introductions were made.

Louisa Escobar was far from old, and anything but crusty. Five foot seven, raven-haired and olive-skinned in line with her Hispanic background, she could easily have made her living as a fashion model if she hadn't gone in for fighting crime. The skirt and blouse she wore were both conservatively cut, but there was no good way to hide the luscious figure underneath.

"Good morning, Mr. Gray."

"A pleasure, Sergeant Escobar."

"Not yet. I'm short on time."

"Of course. Let's get right down to business, then."

"Which is?"

"As I explained to your lieutenant on the telephone, I'm an attorney. I've been retained by the Delgado family—"

"Who?"

"Delgado. Out of Ensenada. Their son, Miguel, was one of the victims in your case."

"A wet?" she asked.

"An innocent, as far as I'm concerned. He certainly did nothing that rated summary execution."

"Agreed," the sergeant said. "I must admit I'm curious on one point, Counselor."

"Feel free."

"This family in Ensenada. How could they afford your services? How would they even know to get in touch?"

"The contact wasn't difficult. They have friends on this side of the border, and I've handled various cases in the barrio over the past two years. As far as fees go, this one is *pro bono*. I'll be paid if there's recovery in a civil action."

"Who's the defendant?"

Johnny smiled. "That's one reason I'm here. If you've got any suspects—"

"Counselor, you know I'm not at liberty to share that kind of information. If and when we make arrests, you'll have a chance to get in line."

"I guess you've heard about the witness, then."

There was a flicker in the sergeant's eyes, a combination of suspicion and alarm.

"What witness would that be?"

"You mean you haven't heard?"

"Counselor, if you've got something to say, let's hear it."

"Well, I'm not sure. Besides, I don't have solid sources."

"Does the phrase 'obstructing justice' ring a bell?"

"I'm not here to give you any grief, Sergeant."

"All right, I'm listening."

"Just this—the word along the border has it that one slipped through the noose. Might put a finger on the shooters, given half a chance."

"You picked this up by word of mouth?"

"Somebody tipped my clients off," he told her, steering clear of Eddie Lopez and the rest of it. "No details on ID, unfortunately. I was thinking that with your connections maybe you could run it down."

"Assuming there's anything to it."

"It's worth a look, I'd say...unless you're onto something better."

"Word from Mexico, that was?"

"It's all I have to offer you right now."

"You understand how thin this is."

"At least it's something."

"Maybe, maybe not."

"Of course, if you're not interested..."

"I didn't say that, Counselor. I'd like to speak with your clients."

Johnny shook his head. "They're not inclined to chat with the authorities right now."

"Why not?"

He understood the risks involved and played his hole card, anyway.

"Because the word is that the triggers came in uniform."

"What?"

"You heard me right."

Her face turned stony. "Counselor, that sounds an awful lot like someone's desperate attempt to nail the county on a suit for wrongful death."

"I wouldn't know until I find that witness," Johnny answered.

"This is a continuing police investigation. You'd be ill-advised to interfere and play detective on your own."

"Somebody has to follow up on active information, Sergeant."

"Right. That's our job."

"Absolutely. If you do it."

"Mr.—"

"Gray," he finished for her, adding, "John."

"Mr. Gray, I don't appreciate a stranger waltzing in here and accusing me—or this department—of participation in a cover-up."

"No accusations, Sergeant. I'm just covering my bets, that's all. If we assume there's one chance in a thousand of police complicity...well, how should I know if it's metro, county, CHP, whatever?"

"Or a total hoax," she snapped. "Assuming there *is* a witness, which you haven't proved by any means, the rest of it is third- or fourth-hand gossip off the streets. Cops catch a lot of heat these days. You know that. Some of it checks out okay, but mostly it's hot air. Somebody has a grudge against the badge, or wants to bargain charges down by countering with accusations of brutality. It happens every day."

"That's why I'm here," he told her. "If my mind was made up, I'd be having this conversation with the FBI."

"So you're just dropping off a tip, is that it?"

"I'm requesting help. If I turn something up, I'll pass it on direct to you. If you turn up that witness, I'd appreciate a call."

"You have a card?" she asked at last.

He passed it over. Office numbers and the answering exchange where she could leave a message, any time of night or day.

"No promises," the sergeant told him, dropping the business card onto her desk.

"I hope to be in touch," he answered. "One way or another."

"Just don't get in the detectives' way."

"I'll do my best."

Outside he checked the mental scoreboard, calling it a draw. It was a risky game, provoking the authorities when they were high on his list of suspects, but he had considered all the angles of attack before he made his move. This way, if anyone was spying on him, following his movements, he would be prepared.

As for his brother, Johnny saw no problem.

Mack was born prepared.

HE FOUND A PUBLIC BOOTH on Clairemont Mesa Boulevard, the telephone still functioning, although the adjacent filling station had long since been abandoned, earmarked for demolition. His target list included several private numbers for Sylvester Ramos, and Bolan chose the one marked Home as he thumbed a quarter into the slot.

There were three rings before a gruff voice answered on the other end. "Who is this?"

"Could be a friend. Put Ramos on the line."

"There ain't no Ramos here."

"I'll bet your life there is."

"Suppose you're wrong?"

"Then I suppose we couldn't talk about his recent losses."

"Hold the phone a minute, will you?"

"Make it fast. I haven't got all day."

A different voice came back at Bolan forty seconds later. "Who is this?"

"I played that game already with your gofer. Names won't help you."

"Who says I need any help?"

"I could be wrong," the Executioner replied. "Could be you like to get your ass kicked three or four times a day."

"If there's a point to this, let's hear it."

"You've been taking hits. I thought you might be curious about the reason."

"Say you're right. You got the answers?"

"Maybe someone doesn't like the way you've grown so fast. Could be they think the border's still an open territory."

"So?"

"So you've been flexing heavy muscle lately, getting into other people's faces with your ego trip. That business with the wets a few nights back was bad for everybody."

"I don't follow you." There was a cutting edge to Ramos's voice.

"Okay, you say so. I'm just playing messenger. No skin off me if you want to try a suicide."

"Fuck you. Nobody tells me where to go or what to do."

"It never crossed my mind," Bolan said. "I just thought you'd like to know why you're about to die."

"You bastard!"

"Temper, temper. You should try to keep your head clear for the next few hours, anyway. It may be all the time you have."

"We'll see."

"Yeah, I guess we will. Good luck."

He cradled the receiver, smiling to himself. Let Ramos stew for a while, considering the list of enemies that Bolan estimated must be several pages long. How many people had the dealer stepped on coming up, or even in the past twelve months? Some of them were still alive, no doubt, and others lost to families who paid their debts in blood.

And when he finished counting enemies, Sylvester could begin to take a fresh look at his friends, subordinates, suppliers... anyone at all, in short, who stood to profit by his sudden death.

If he got nervous, great. A nervous player sometimes made mistakes that brought him down. And if Sylvester's nerve held out, at least he would be busy looking over his shoulder, waiting for the next blow to fall.

But never knowing when or where.

Bolan held the initiative in that department, and he was just getting started.

LOUISA ESCOBAR WAS worried, even if she didn't let it show. Her visitor, this lawyer—John Gray?—had set some ugly wheels in motion, churning up her darkest thoughts and ruining whatever chance she had at getting through the day with peace of mind intact.

She'd been working on the desert massacre for four straight days without a break. They knew the victims' names, but all the relatives they could identify were back in Mexico, effectively beyond her reach. A string of conversations with the Federal Judicial Police had turned up nothing in the way of leads, and there was nothing she could do to get the *federales* moving any faster, even if she had proof they were dogging it.

Of course, it was a long shot at the very best, expecting any leads from Mexico. It wasn't as if the wets were anybody special, with the kind of enemies who put out contracts for a murder using hit men and machine guns. They were simple peasants, laborers and such. Undoubtedly a few of them were leaving grudges in their native land, perhaps an argument worth killing over, but she didn't buy the link.

As for the coyote, Serafino Alvarez, he could have been involved in damn near anything, from drugs to gunrunning, when he wasn't herding wets across the border. These characters were strictly mercenary, all the way, and you could figure every one of them had fingers in at least a dozen different pies. Unfortunately Alvarez appeared to have no family or friends at all, according to the last report of the *federales*.

The case had taken something out of Escobar to start with. Her own grandfather had been a wetback in the Great Depression when California's megaranchers used Mexican stoop labor at prices even starving Anglos would reject. It had been something close to slavery in those days, but he'd made it through and somehow raised a family. His sons—Louisa's father among them—were all naturalized citizens by the time they'd come of age, a new world opening before them.

But the new world still had many of the same old problems. Racial prejudice to start with. Unemployment. Poverty. Police who used their sticks and pistols first, asking questions later...when they asked at all. Louisa was the first girl in her family to finish high school, later working nights to put herself through two years of city college. She loved athletics, had a craving for adventure and was conscious of the universal shortfall when it came to justice in the world.

So she became a cop. Or, more precisely, a sheriff's deputy. Taking full advantage of the various hiring programs for women and minorities, she pulled every string she could reach to nail the job, confident that she could prove herself worthy once she got the badge and uniform secured.

And so she had.

A two-year sergeant at the age of thirty-one, she was on track with her career, intent on wearing a lieutenant's bars before her thirty-fifth birthday. From there who could say? She didn't think that San Diego County was prepared to elect a female Hispanic sheriff, but there were other avenues of advancement open, once she secured a command rank in the department. Even going back to school wasn't beyond the realm of possibility.

But at the moment she had murder on her hands, and interference from a lawyer who was causing her to question the department that she served.

She'd been right about his story: it was hearsay, start to finish. "Someone said" there was a witness to the massacre, and "someone said the witness said" the shooters were police. No mention of specific agencies or jurisdiction, nothing in the way of physical descriptions.

Zip.

She'd considered passing it to her lieutenant, but she knew what he would say. What any veteran cop would say, confronted with a tale like that.

Forget it.

First off, she didn't know this lawyer. Fifty-fifty he was either looking for an easy score in civil court to soak some victim's family for a percentage of the take, or he was into "civil liberties," intent on making the police look bad at any cost to truth and justice. Either way she had to take his story with at least a pound of salt unless hard evidence turned up to verify a witness's existence in the case.

And if the witness *did* exist, she hit the second thorny line of problems. Gray had given her no name, sex, address, physical description, nothing. The location of the massacre told Escobar that a survivor would most likely run back home to Baja, putting him—or her—effectively beyond the reach of county officers. Supposing that she learned enough to track down the so-called witness, they'd be dealing with the standard problems of identifying suspects seen at night on unfamiliar turf and in circumstances that were certainly traumatic at the very least. The odds against a firm ID were astronomical.

She ought to wipe the whole thing from her mind at once and concentrate on solid evidence. The problem being that the solid evidence led nowhere, leaving her completely at loose ends.

They knew the gunmen had been packing automatic weapons. Three 9 mm submachine guns had been used to snuff out fifteen lives, and they could make the weapons easily enough with a ballistics test . . . if they could ever find the guns. Until that time, however, they were screwed.

Local newspapers had already given up on the case, recognizing a dead-end story when they saw one. If the body count had been a little smaller, it would probably have missed the national media entirely, and none of the network reports showed any interest after four days of no comment from the sheriff's office.

Fifteen dead, and after four days marking time, she almost felt like giving up. It troubled her, that feeling, but Louisa recognized the problem. San Diego's clearance rate for homicide was in the crapper, based in part on transient population problems and the border's proximity. She understood that there was only so much she could do.

The part she didn't—wouldn't—understand was poor police work: so-called homicide detectives writing off the murder of a hooker or a homosexual because the victims "didn't rate"; suspicious suicides and accidents that barely caught a second glance from trained professionals; a general tendency to let things slide.

It wasn't institutional corruption in the ordinary sense. Instead, she traced the problem to a feeling of defeat, engendered by too many years of revolving-door justice in the court system, too much emphasis on the sacred rights of felons, all at the expense of decent working cops and injured victims. Any job had burnouts in direct proportion to the stress and frustration endured from day to day. Some quit, a few more ate their guns, and some decided they could coast through twenty years no sweat, just going through the motions, signing off on easy cases and allowing all the rest to go unsolved.

Not this time.

Fourteen wets and one coyote might not matter to the system, but Louisa Escobar had a personal interest in the case. It was part of her history, part of her life, and she wouldn't let go that easily. She owed those strangers and the people she worked for a solution to the mystery.

There might not be a witness to the massacre, but she would have to check it out. If she discovered that her visitor, John Gray, was working on some kind of scam, it would be her enduring pleasure to arrest him for obstructing justice, filing false reports and any other charge she could think of. Maybe even see his ass disbarred.

But if his story checked . . .

Well, she'd have to wait and see. Too early yet for her to plan beyond the moment. She'd have to take it one step at time, and that meant going to the streets, touching base with her network of eyes and ears in the barrio.

Just like old times.

She picked up her tailored jacket and headed for the door.

6

A major part of rattling any enemy was giving him diverse targets to work with, dividing his attention and thereby reducing the odds of a lucky, coincidental hit. With that in mind the Executioner decided it was time to shift his focus, easing up in one direction, bearing down in another.

First up, one Rico Escalante, half of the surviving brother act that had been vexing Ramos in the realm of cocaine smuggling and sales. The brothers had a heavy grudge against Sylvester as it was, and Bolan guessed it would take only a minor shove to put them on the verge of open war.

Assuming they kept up on current events, the Escalantes had to know that Ramos had been taking major heat since sunrise, and they'd be speculating on its source. Confusion fostered paranoia, and the brothers had to estimate that Ramos would be striking back, perhaps in their direction, if he couldn't find another, better target close at hand.

So be it.

Bolan recognized the opening and meant to use it to his own advantage, if he could.

Beginning now.

The younger Escalante had a condominium on Fanta Drive in El Cajón. Security was tight, but Bolan didn't plan on dropping in for a chat. He had something different in mind. Maximum shock value with minimal risk to himself in the process. A perfect sideshow to the coming main event.

He parked downrange from Escalante's condo on the opposite side of the street and took a heavy toolbox from the back seat of his car. The coveralls he wore were nondescript, the perfect outfit for a working man. He strolled along the sidewalk to the stylish building facing Rico's. Then in through the lobby, where a doorman lounged behind a wooden desk.

"Help you?"

"The other way around. I'm here to fix that air conditioner."

"I didn't know we had a problem."

Bolan shrugged. "I just go where I'm told."

The doorman checked his clipboard, ran an index finger down the list on top and shook his head. "There's nothing here."

"Okay, friend, you're the man." He reached inside the pocket of his coveralls and drew a piece of folded paper out. "You won't mind signing off that I was here and tried to do my job."

"Hang on a sec. I didn't say you couldn't do it."

"So?"

"Service elevator on your left. It'll take you all the way to the roof."

"Obliged."

He rode the elevator up and punched a button that would hold it there, doors open wide, until he finished on the roof. Not long if all went well. A simple in-and-out with time to spare.

He circled the elevator housing quickly, moving toward the street side of the building. There he had an unobstructed view of Escalante's penthouse windows. The draperies were open, welcoming the sunlight, but their mirror finish blocked his view of anyone inside.

No sweat.

He hadn't come to kill, although he would happily take out Escalante if the opportunity arose. Instead, it would be basic rattling for effect, and if he scored a lucky hit along the way, so much the better.

Bolan knelt and opened his toolbox, lifting out the removable tray with its screwdrivers, pliers and other items. Underneath, the lever-action Marlin .444 Magnum lay in two pieces, waiting to be reassembled. He made the fitting quickly, skillfully, double-checking the rifle's load before he raised it to his shoulder and sighted through the sniper scope.

Escalante's mirrored windows sprang into sharp relief, Bolan tracking from left to right and back again. No openings, no view of anyone behind the one-way glass. He picked a giant pane at random, worked the Marlin's lever to chamber a live round and settled into the squeeze.

It stood to reason that the windows would be double-thick at least, perhaps intended to be bulletproof. If nothing else, at least the Magnum armor-piercing rounds would leave their mark behind and give the Escalante brothers something to consider over lunch.

Like hitting back at Ramos, for example.

Bolan took a deep breath, released half of it and held the rest. His finger took up slack on the Marlin's trigger, even as he braced himself to absorb the powerful recoil.

One away, and thunder in his ears. Across the street a fist-size hole appeared in Escalante's window, granting Bolan a quick glimpse inside. His second round took half the window out, the glass exploding into fragments, showering the room beyond.

He swiveled, firing rapidly until the rifle's five rounds were expended and the penthouse had a single window left intact. He thought about reloading but decided he was out of time, the numbers falling. Escalante's people would be mounting a response in moments, and he didn't want a firefight here and now.

Mere seconds were required to dismantle the Marlin and stow it in his toolbox. He backtracked to the waiting service elevator, cleared the lock and rode it down. The doorman looked surprised to see him as he moved in the direction of the street. "You done already?"

Bolan shook his head and smiled. "I haven't even started yet."

SYLVESTER RAMOS considered ripping his telephone out of the wall and hurling it into the swimming pool, but he knew that it would be a childish thing to do. Machismo called for action, granted, but the action must be well thought out, deliberate . . . and above all else, mature.

No screaming tantrums for the man who sought to dominate both San Diego and the nearby strip of border territory. If he let his enemies reduce him to a childlike state, he was as good as dead.

A drink, then.

Ramos favored rum and Coke, but this time he ignored the Coke. A blast of fire against his tonsils, then the spreading warmth he knew so well. Not peace of mind exactly, but the next best thing in crisis situations.

Calm.

He needed time to think, but that could be a problem. Three hits in as many hours, and the warning call from who-knows-who to tip him off that he had enemies. As if that would come as a surprise to anyone with brains enough to tie their shoes.

The problem was, he had too many enemies. Right there in San Diego, he was rumbling with the Escalante brothers, squeezing out small-fry and demanding tribute payments from the men who made their living running wets across the line. All kinds of enemies, for starters, but he wouldn't have suspected any of them had the skill—much less the nerve—to strike at him this way with such tenacity.

Across the border there were friends and enemies, one as trustworthy as the other. He did business with the Aguelo family and the Cortez brothers on a regular basis, but that wouldn't prevent either or both of the gangs from trying to expand, perhaps eliminate Sylvester and absorb the territory he had eked out for himself these past few years. Again his enemies would number several dozen small-time dealers, maybe hundreds of coyotes who had felt the pinch of tribute payments recently. He had no doubt that any one of them would kill him, given half a chance, but few—if any—had the weapons, cash or brains to orchestrate a string of hits like he had suffered since the crack of dawn.

Luis Calvada was dead, his largest cutting plant destroyed, with close to eighty kilos up in smoke. One of his favorite clubs had been demolished by a bomb. Nine lives in all so far, and he got sick just thinking of the cost.

He had two gringo whores from the Calvada murder and a pair of kitchen workers from the club, all glad to spill their guts when they found out who they were talking to. One coked-out bitch had slept right through Luis's death, but her companion offered a description of a tall, dark man, civilian clothes, some kind of automatic weapon with a silencer. The fry cooks gave a similar description, all except for the machine gun. Their man had been carrying an automatic and some kind of bag across his shoulder, no doubt with the bomb inside.

They all agreed the shooter was an Anglo, on the dark side, possibly Italian. That made Ramos think about the Mafia, but he had made his peace with the Castiglione Family three years earlier. The first twelve months he had paid them five percent of his earnings to keep the Family off his back. From that point on he had enough guns and muscle that he didn't feel like paying anymore. The bastards sent a crew around to see him, as expected, and he sent them back in sandwich bags, all sliced and diced. He'd had no problem with the Family since then, and he suspected they were secretly relieved to ditch the cocaine traffic, with its crazy Indians and rip-offs and high-noon shoot-outs on the street, as if they were in some kind of psycho western movie.

Ramos would have cut it loose himself, except for two things. First, the profits were incredible. And second, he sincerely loved his work.

Except today.

The latest call had been a puzzler, throwing him off-stride. Someone had tried a hit on Rico Escalante at his penthouse, blowing out the windows with some kind of cannon the way they did in the movies. No one was hit apparently, but not for lack of trying. And the shooter had evaporated, getting clean away.

It changed things, in Ramos's way of thinking, when his rivals started taking hits. He didn't know who had pulled the trigger on the Escalante raid, except that it was no one he employed. The brothers might have other enemies, of course—it would be something of a miracle if they didn't—but Ramos viewed the timing with extreme suspicion. It was almost as if . . .

What?

As if someone were trying to provoke a war in San Diego. A couple of hits on Ramos, then a raid against the Escalante brothers, just to keep things rolling. Make each side believe the other was responsible, and then sit back and watch while they engaged each other, fighting to the death.

His thoughts returned to the Castiglione Family, but he couldn't imagine any of them coming up with such a convoluted plan. It played like something from a James Bond movie, but it just might work, if the intended targets lost their heads.

It struck him that he ought to try to call the Escalante brothers, let them know that he wasn't behind the hit on Rico, but he couldn't bring himself to do it. Not yet. The brothers almost certainly would blame him for the shooting, and they might retaliate, but he'd face that problem when it came. Right now his mind was focused on the nameless enemy who had appeared from nowhere, challenging the new King of the Border to an all-out war.

Old man Aguelo had the brains to lay a plan like this if he stayed sober long enough. It was a possibility that Ramos would investigate without delay. If he found out his allies had betrayed him, it wouldn't go well for the Aguelos. Hell, he might decide to rub them out regardless and absorb their contact with the Colombians. It couldn't hurt to buy the shit direct instead of dealing through a greedy middleman.

But he was getting sidetracked now. The surest way to beat an enemy was to anticipate his moves and head him off, surprise him with an ambush where he least expected it. The trouble was, you had to know your enemy before you had a prayer of getting in his head and seeing things through his eyes, scoping out the way he laid his plans and learning the weak spots. Until they found out who this bastard was they might as well be shadowboxing in a basement with the lights turned off.

Ramos poured himself another shot of rum and drank it down.

He needed information before he went to war. And that meant calling on his friends in uniform. A simple favor for the man who paid their second, unreported salaries.

It was the very least that they could do.

7

By half past noon Louisa Escobar was getting worried. She had started out all right, a combination of skepticism and irritation, anxious to disprove the lawyer's cockeyed story, but the past three hours had turned her mood around.

She'd been working her informants right through lunchtime, checking out the barrio for starters. Her connection with the people had been strained when she put on a badge, but she'd worked to get it back, taking full advantage of her ethnic background and department perks to forge new links with the community. It was rough going for a while, but she proved herself in situations where discretion was required. She didn't throw her weight around or lord it over the community, harassing wets and homeboys just to prove herself the way some Mexican-Americans in uniform felt honor-bound to do. A certain trust had been established in the process, with Louisa proving she could keep her word. But some barrio residents still regarded her as a sellout *tia taco*—the Hispanic equivalent of an Uncle Tom—and they would lie to her without a second thought. Some would doubtless kill her, given half a chance.

Louisa knew her snitches, though, and she could tell when they were lying to her. Generally, at least. This morning everything they told her had the eerie ring of truth.

The desert massacre of four nights back was still a topic of persistent conversation in the San Diego barrio. Louisa's people were accustomed to the daily toll of violence, self-inflicted and official, but this kind of slaughter was something else again. It went beyond the casual disregard for human life that marked so many barrio transactions.

There was calculated viciousness in this, a new level of savagery that left even her hardened street sources in a kind of awe. They spoke to her reluctantly at first, but they had spoken.

Half a dozen times she heard the story of a witness to the massacre, although none of her informants could agree on sex or age. One told her the survivor was a child, two others said a woman, and the last three confidently said it was a man. Two thought the witness was in San Diego, one suggested she had made it to Los Angeles, and three believed the answer lay in Mexico.

There was little Louisa could do with such jumbled, contradictory reports, but they gave added weight to the lawyer's report. If he was truly representing clients on the far side of the border, that made four votes for her witness hiding out in Baja.

Wait a second.

She was wise enough to know how rumors traveled in the barrio, or anywhere. It could be total bullshit, and the whole community would "know" a hundred different versions of the "facts" this time next week. How many times in her career had she been sidetracked by erroneous reports of the suspects, evidence, narcotics shipments and the like?

Too many.

Still, it was the kind of information she couldn't dismiss without a closer look. Especially when she took the other rumors into consideration.

Thirteen of her snitches, including all six who reported a massacre survivor, claimed police had been involved in the killings. Three reported confidently that authorities arrested the victims as they were crossing the border, then turned them over to an unofficial firing squad. The rest were equally insistent that police had pulled the triggers for themselves.

In every case but one a hot-shit dealer named Sylvester Ramos had been fingered as the man behind the massacre.

Assuming it was true, it had to be the perfect crime. When every member of a target population knew you were guilty, and police were stymied for a solid lead to make the case in court, you had the makings of a reputation that left a dealer's enemies in awe.

She wanted to dismiss the stories out of hand, but she couldn't afford professional myopia at this stage of the game. The problem was exactly where to go with what she had.

She had tried to pin her sources down to a department, starting with the Border Patrol and working her way down the list of state and local agencies, but all in vain. They simply shrugged and put her off with the advice that one cop was the same as any other...present company excluded, of course.

Louisa wasn't ready to accept the rumors as established fact, not yet, but she had heard enough to make her wary. She couldn't afford to blunder through the next phase of her investigation, stepping on toes and perhaps getting herself killed in the bargain. If cops *were* involved—and she had seen enough the past few years to stop short of closing her mind to the prospect—then she'd have to be doubly careful with each move she made from this point on.

If she spilled what she knew, or what she was beginning to suspect, to the wrong person, she was asking for trouble. Maybe the killing kind. Before she took another step Louisa had to know exactly where she was going and how to get there.

Above all else, who could she trust?

Her supervisor was Lieutenant Darren Lassiter, a twenty-year veteran with the sheriff's department who had an exemplary record. To be sure, he carried some of the traditional male macho baggage common to most veteran cops, but he had never tried to sell her short because of sex or race, as far as she could tell. The alternative, if she didn't speak with Lassiter, would be a trip to internal affairs... and the last thing Louisa wanted at the moment was to saddle herself with a team of head-hunters looking for street cops to crucify.

The more she thought about it, taking the reports to her lieutenant seemed the way to go.

Beginning now.

THE RADIO KEPT Johnny current on his brother's progress, new accounts of "violence in the drug trade" coming in with hourly reports of weather, traffic and the latest news from Washington. Police were blaming all of it on unnamed cocaine smugglers, promising arrests without delay.

Good luck.

Sylvester Ramos had been running heavy shipments through the heart of San Diego for the past four years, at least, without a major interruption by authorities. His string of drug-related murders had remained unsolved, except for one case where a shooter he had employed was stupid enough to make the hit in public with patrolmen half a block away. On that occasion, though, the gunner had fought it out and died with his boots on, preventing homicide detectives from interrogating him about the man who pulled his strings.

So much for swift solutions.

He had considered hanging out around the courthouse for a while, waiting to see if Sergeant Escobar rose to his bait, but the move was too risky in more ways than one. He didn't need to take the chance of winding up in jail for following a cop on her appointed rounds, nor did he wish to be caught napping if his brother needed him.

He had a walkie-talkie and a CB in his car, but simple contact and a suitable response were very different things. If Mack touched base and needed help, he wouldn't have the time to spare while Johnny drove back home, picked up his gear and made his way to a selected rendezvous. It was a risk just leaving Strongbase long enough to meet with Sergeant Escobar, and part of him was glad to get back home.

Mixed feelings, really, when he thought about it. Waiting was the pits when he'd rather be out there, fighting at his brother's side. Mack did his best to minimize their fieldwork, even recognizing Johnny's capability and training. Part of it was superstition, he imagined, an ingrained fear of putting the last two Bolan eggs in one shaky basket, but at least it came from caring.

Even so it got on Johnny's nerves.

How many times had he been close to death since his release from military service? The adult reunion with his brother had been fraught with peril, but he'd finally impressed on Mack the fact that he couldn't be sent to bed without his supper like a child. He wouldn't find himself a safe and sane profession, hiding out behind another name while Mack took all the risks. The loss that tore their lives apart had also welded them together; it belonged to both of them, and not just to the Executioner.

A part of Johnny longed to ditch his legal practice, leave it flat and run away to Stony Man and take assignments on his own, if Mack was too concerned about the risks of working as a team. He knew Brognola would be as mad as hell, might even turn him down, but there was more involved with Johnny staying put than simple fear of failure.

He was also doing something with his life.

The cases that he handled rarely made the headlines, and a number of them passed without a ripple in the media. The past six months he'd negotiated seven civil rights claims to successful settlements, and he was working on harassment of the homeless by police and vigilantes. Unlike some self-proclaimed "civil libertarians," he didn't feel compelled to work for trash. He had ejected Nazi skinheads from the office once, sending three to emergency receiving, and his hard-line stance on pimps and dealers was well-known on the streets. Conversely, when a battered working girl had come in to ask for an injunction that would stop her "man" from beating her, Johnny managed to settle the case out of court. That weekend Sammy Sugar had been awakened from his boozy slumber by a man dressed in black who shoved a Smith & Wesson pistol into his mouth and dropped a not-so-subtle invitation for the pimp to find himself another town.

Word got around.

The Ramos gig was something else, though. Until they had some solid evidence in hand he was looking at a gang involved in major drug sales, probable mass murder and police corruption on a scale he could only guess. The more he learned about Sylvester Ramos from his sources on the street, the more it seemed to Johnny that his first report from Eddie Lopez might be accurate.

He didn't have to leave Strongbase to connect with many of his sources. Some of them preferred the telephone, as long as they could make the call from friendly turf. It saved them meeting face-to-face with anyone who might bring heat down on their heads, and names were never used in case the line was tapped from one end or the other.

So far, since the Lopez hit, three other sources had confirmed the rumor of a witness to the desert massacre. This morning, shortly after meeting with Louisa Escobar, he had received yet another message from the streets. This latest lead sounded solid, with the caller saying that the answer lay in Tijuana.

Worth a look perhaps, but he'd have to get in touch with Mack before he made a border run and left Strongbase unattended. Timing and coordination made a military action work, and he wasn't about to leave his brother stranded on a whim.

Which only left the basic rudiments of touching base. While Mack could call him on the telephone or radio at any time, there was no guaranteed secure procedure for dispatching messages the other way. His brother would be moving constantly, keeping his enemies off balance, and distraction could be fatal.

Johnny knew he'd have to wait his turn, but in the meantime he could put some feelers out and try to find out what was happening around him.

Waiting was the worst part, but he had no choice.

When Mack was ready for him, Johnny knew there would be heat enough to go around.

RAMON IBARRA WAS A trigger for Sylvester Ramos, one of two or three the dealer trusted with his really tough assignments. His condominium was a long stride from the local barrio, and Bolan figured that the contract shooter liked it that way. Sudden riches sometimes prompted criminals to overemphasize their ethnic roots, but others—like Ibarra—looked for distance from the squalor that was home. They weren't intent on "going Anglo," really, more concerned with washing off the stink of poverty and living up to standards they had learned from years of watching movies and TV commercials. Flashy cars and stylish women, maybe a whirlpool in the bathroom, and a wall safe stuffed with cash.

All the comforts of home.

Bolan took a chance and slipped in through the service entrance, going up six flights of stairs to bypass the elevator in the lobby, where the doorman would have made his face. On three he found Ibarra's door and palmed the 93-R with its custom silencer attached.

It never hurt to be prepared.

No one answered on the first ring, and muffled cursing came from beyond the door when Bolan rang again.

"Hang on a fuckin' minute, will you?"

The warrior heard the sound of footsteps moving closer, slow and heavy. "Who?" a voice asked. There was no peephole in the door, a fatal oversight.

"Jésus. Sylvester sent me over, man. You ready?"

"Ready?"

Ibarra fumbled at the dead bolt, then opened the door a crack. The chain allowed him something like two inches, and one eye peered through at Bolan, blinking with a total lack of recognition.

"Hey, I don't know you."

One kick was all it took to break the chain and slam the door into Ibarra's face. He tumbled backward, stunned, and Bolan was inside the condo by the time his eyes began to focus.

He was quick, though. Bolan gave him that. A lurching twist, and he was scrabbling away on hands and knees in the direction of a shotgun propped against an easy chair. He almost made it, one hand stretching out to grab the weapon when a Parabellum mangler clipped his right knee from behind and turned it into bloody pulp.

Ibarra roared in pain as he landed facedown on the deep shag carpet. Scuttling forward on his elbows and his one good knee, he reached the 12-gauge just as Bolan fired again. The second Parabellum round ripped through Ibarra's shoulder joint and dropped him onto his face again, the shotgun toppling out of reach.

Enough.

Bolan moved up beside him, kicking the shotgun farther away before he holstered the Beretta and reached down to lift Ibarra by his collar and belt. He dropped the wounded hitter into the easy chair and stepped back a pace.

"Can you hear me, Ramón?"

The gunner raised his head. "I hear."

"I've got a message for Sylvester. How's your memory?"

"I hear you."

It was close enough.

"The message is, he's going out of business. He's been stepping on too many toes. It's time to pay. You got that?"

"Out of business. Time to pay."

He took the shotgun with him, just in case, and left it in the service stairwell. A surprise for the custodian next time around.

The message would get through, or most of it at any rate, if Ibarra didn't bleed to death before he reached the telephone. He had fair odds, and more than he deserved.

It was a short walk to his car, and Bolan made it easily. Behind the wheel he took a moment to unwind.

And it was time to make another call.

8

Louisa Escobar felt nervous as she made her way to the lieutenant's office, typewriters and voices keeping up a steady background noise in the squad room around her. She had called ahead for the appointment before returning to the courthouse, and the drive had given her time to think.

It was the right move, she repeated to herself. Internal affairs was a write-off from the start, and her only alternative—tackling the problem on her own—offered the slimmest of hopes for a viable solution.

On her own she could expect resistance from both sides, and she knew where her first loyalty lay. The department had given her a new shot at life, a way out of the barrio, and while she recognized the cold, hard facts of bigotry, occasional brutality and isolated cases of corruption, she wasn't prepared to throw her new life off that easily. It would require a damn sight more than rumors off the street before she turned on everything that she had worked for, everything that she believed in.

Lieutenant Darren Lassiter was forty-four years old and could have passed for ten years younger on his better days. He kept himself in shape and had the reputation of a ladies' man since his divorce three years earlier. He didn't hit on lady cops, however, and his treatment of Louisa since her transfer into homicide had been strictly professional. She sometimes got the feeling that he wished she was a man, but Lassiter had never faulted her for her performance.

Until now.

She was about to hit him with a story he wouldn't appreciate, and there was no way of predicting how he might react. Disbelief, for starters, and beyond that...

She knocked on the door of Lassiter's office, receiving a brisk "Come" in return. The lieutenant kept a tidy desk, with manila file folders neatly stacked to one side, an unsorted pile of reports on the other. Lassiter stayed in his seat as she entered, waving her toward an empty chair that sat facing the desk. "Have a seat, Sergeant."

"Thank you, sir."

"I haven't got a lot of time to spare these days. You made it sound important on the phone."

"Yes, sir, I think it just might be."

"Let's hear it, then."

"About this business in the desert, sir..."

"I'm listening."

"My snitches are reporting a survivor."

Lassiter frowned and cocked an eyebrow at her, questioning. "A name?"

She shook her head. "Not yet. I'm hoping, but it may still take some time."

"More likely it's a line of bullshit."

"I don't think so, sir."

"Why not?"

"A feeling. Nothing I can pin it on right now, but no one's offering to sell me the specifics. If it was a lot of crap, I would have looked for someone trying to cash in."

"That's pretty shaky, Sergeant."

"Yes, sir, but I think it's worth a check."

"There's nothing else?"

She took a breath, considering, and knew she would have to give him something more to make it work. "I'm hearing that Sylvester Ramos is behind the killings."

"Ramos?" Lassiter seemed honestly surprised. "We don't have anything to link this job with dope. Somebody's feeding you a line."

"I'd like to run it down."

"You've got a full load as it is, correct?"

"I've made the massacre priority."

"It may be time to reevaluate that choice."

"Lieutenant?"

"Four days on a wetback killing, Sergeant. I don't have to quote the stats on homicide solutions, do I? Anything beyond forty-eight hours, it's a miracle if we solve it at all."

"With fifteen people dead—"

"And not one solid motive in the batch that we can lay our hands on."

"That's why I believe we ought to take a closer look at Ramos."

"What's the angle?" Lassiter inquired.

"From what I hear, extortion. Word I get, Sylvester has been doing everything he can to nail the border down. All traffic, wets included. Tribute going either way. I'm hearing Alvarez refused to pay him off, so Ramos had to pay him back."

"My best advice to you would be forget it, Sergeant. Still, if you're convinced there's something to it go ahead—within reason. I don't want your other cases suffering due to some fixation on Ramos."

"No, sir."

Already on her feet, she knew it was her final chance to drop the other shoe, explain the rumors of police involvement in the murders, but she held the information back. Lassiter was skeptical enough as it was without her taking any shots at anonymous guys on the job.

"You'll keep me up-to-date?"

"Of course, sir."

Moving through the squad room to her desk, she waited for the first rush of relief to tell her she had made it past one obstacle.

Just one.

The easy part was all behind her now, and she would have to see about unraveling a snarl of rumors on her own.

LASSITER POURED HIMSELF a cup of coffee and returned to his desk, rocking back in the swivel chair, a dark frown carving furrows in his face. He felt the faint beginnings of a headache and checked his pulse from force of habit, an automatic reflex from the old days when he played team sports in college.

Take care of your body, and your body would take care of you.

Unless some sneaky bastard came around and stabbed you in the back.

The interview with Escobar had left his nerves on edge, his stomach sour. Normally he only felt that way when he was visiting his in-laws, or when the IA headhunters were prowling around his division, looking for good cops to crucify. This time, however, his anxiety had a more pressing cause.

If Escobar kept digging, who knew what she might come up with? All this talk of witnesses, Sylvester Ramos and the rest of it made Lassiter extremely nervous.

Damn it, anyway.

When his superiors sent a woman down to homicide—a Mexican at that—he swallowed it the way he'd swallowed all the other orders in his long career. There seemed to be no point in making waves and bringing heat upon himself when he could simply watch and wait. If Escobar made out, terrific. If she screwed up once or twice, he'd be ready for her, running her evaluations down and passing word upstairs that she didn't seem capable of carrying her weight.

As things worked out, the lady did her job efficiently and made Lassiter's division look good in the process. She'd nabbed a guy killing women out in Claremont, broken up a ring that killed old codgers for their life insurance and personally nailed a Baptist minister who had tried to make the murder of his wife look like an accident. In short, she knew her business, and she kept it simple when the press rolled out their microphones and videocameras, chapter and verse down the line, with a firm "No comment" in all the right places.

Lassiter had grown to like the only woman on his squad, but that was personal, and private feelings never carried any weight where business was concerned. No matter how much he admired the lady, Lassiter could not—would not—allow her to destroy the perfect setup he had managed for himself.

The witness story was a bunch of crap, he figured. Any time a sensational crime rolled around, you heard a lot of rumors afterward. Bobby Kennedy's girl in the polka-dot dress. Members of the SLA emerging from CIA mind control experiments as full-blown revolutionary psychos. Jimmy Hoffa and Howard Hughes sharing quarters on some tiny Greek island, calling the shots for a worldwide cartel of corruption.

All bullshit, as far as Lassiter was concerned, and he placed Escobar's story of the wetback witness in the same category.

Assuming for a moment that there *was* a witness, what could he or she accomplish in the scheme of things? Some vague descriptions when you factored in the darkness and the panic, maybe nothing more than shadowy shapes with guns. And even that would mean the witness had to surface, come in from the cold and tell his story for the record.

If he—or she—survived that long.

One brush with death was pushing it, Lassiter figured. Twice around would defy all the odds.

Forget about the witness, then. More troubling in the long run had been Escobar's remark about Sylvester Ramos. Lassiter supposed it should have come as no surprise that street talk linked the dealer with San Diego's worst slaughter in nearly a decade. Knowing Ramos, he probably helped spread the word around himself to further the intimidation of his enemies.

Stupid bastard.

Every time you thought he had the program clearly fixed in mind, along came yet another wild card, fished up from the bottom of the deck.

Sylvester wasn't satisfied with the cocaine and grass, couldn't content himself with sixty, maybe sixty-five percent of all the shit that moved through San Diego in a given year. He had to have it all, including wets, gunrunning, chop shops, hookers—any damn thing you could think of that was making money within a fifty-mile radius. Of course, he always asked first; Lassiter would have to give him that much credit.

It was when the answers came back negative that things began to fall apart.

Like now.

How much did Ramos stand to make from a coyote like this Alvarez? Say four, five hundred bills a week. He spent that much on tips at nightclubs, never even felt it, but the ruthless grab for chump change had produced a massacre and brought down heat enough for all concerned. The Feds were looking into it, both Immigration and the FBI, and that was cause enough to worry in itself. Now, if you dropped Louisa Escobar into the pot and let it simmer for a while, you just might end up with a deadly poison brew.

And with the other shit that had been coming down since dawn...

He had a call to make, but the lieutenant didn't trust his office telephone. It might be paranoia, but he also knew enough of office politics to understand that he had enemies out there, disguised as friends. Some of them lusted for his job, while others carried grudges going back for years. A few would simply rather have a more compliant man in homicide, someone who jumped each time he heard their fingers snap.

Good luck.

You had to get up early in the morning if you meant to scam a veteran cop like Darren Lassiter, and you would never do it in his own damn office with a tool as fickle as the telephone.

No way.

He left his office and locked the door behind him, moving toward the elevators. Sedgewick caught him halfway there, a small point on the Jackson murder-suicide, but it was merely a distraction. Part of managing the homicide division in a county where the people seemed to get a real kick out of killing one another day by day.

Downstairs there was a bank of pay phones in the lobby, only one of them in use as he arrived. Some lawyer type, discussing details of a case about to go to trial.

He took the farthest unit down the line and dropped a quarter into the slot, tapping out a number from memory. He recognized the voice that answered on the second ring.

"It's me. We need to talk."

"So talk."

"Not on the phone," Lassiter said. "I've got a problem here, about that business from the other night."

"I've got all kinds of problems."

"Could be they're connected."

"Oh?"

"So do I get the meet, or what?"

"Two hours at the cove."

"Okay."

The line went dead, and Lassiter replaced the handset in its cradle.

MACK BOLAN WATCHED the deli from his vantage point across the street and two doors down. Inside, three gunners from the Ramos family were eating lunch. If any one of them was worried by the prospect of a shooting war, it didn't show.

Machismo, right.

The dealer's hard force would consist primarily of thugs who liked their work—intimidating, maiming, killing other human beings. If a handful nurtured any qualms, they would be sure to hide it from their fellow pistoleros, frightened of displaying weakness that would cast doubt on their manhood, maybe get them killed besides.

He could have bagged all three from where he stood if he was carrying the Marlin, but a noonday firefight with pedestrians involved wasn't on Bolan's list of things to do. Instead, he had a different kind of fireworks show in mind.

The deli was a hit from Johnny's list of possibles, a hangout favored by a certain group of soldiers from the Ramos clan. He'd been hoping for a larger haul, but three would do for now. The cumulative numbers took priority in any battle of attrition, and the Executioner was far from finished yet.

It had been simple to rig up their car. He pegged the gray Mercedes from a list of license plates his brother had supplied, for starters, and the rest was pure audacity. A walk-by in the parking lot, and Bolan dropped his keys, a classic butterfingers, stooping to retrieve them. In a second, give or take, he had attached the flat magnetic parcel underneath the fuel tank, safely out of sight. And scooping up his keys, the clumsy stranger ambled on his way.

After five minutes, he knew he'd have to move. No man on his own spent that much time examining the samples in a jeweler's window, even if he had a foxy babe at home. There was a bookstore down the block, and he could kill more time there, if necessary, but he'd prefer to do the job and move along.

As if on cue, his targets rose and sauntered toward the register, one of them coming onto the female cashier, reaching out to finger her plastic name tag while the others chuckled to themselves and the lady forced a smile.

The hardmen left the deli and looked around as if expecting trouble, which was smart. They didn't bother checking out the Merc, though, which was ultimately a fatal oversight.

He watched them pick their seats, the driver taking time to comb his hair before he reached for the ignition key. They were too close to the deli for Bolan's taste, and he kept his thumb on the trigger switch of the remote-control detonator in his pocket. Let them get some distance, maybe reach the intersection, just so they were well away from innocent civilians.

Traffic in the neighborhood was light, and Bolan's targets had a clear run from the parking lot. He tracked them with his eyes as far as the corner, watching the left-hand turn signal as it started to pulse, the Mercedes slowing, veering gradually to the left.

Okay.

He keyed the switch and saw the rear end of the Merc become airborne, rising on a ball of flame. The gas tank blew so quickly that his ears didn't have time to separate the first blast from the second. The car stood on its nose, then toppled over, blocking the middle of the four-way intersection. The roof was flattened, all the windows shattered by the blast or impact with the street. One tire still spinning, smoking like a pinwheel on the Fourth of July, the rubber melting off in layers.

The Executioner didn't have to check to know the passengers were dead.

Traffic was stalled in all directions. The squad cars, ambulance and fire trucks would have trouble when they got there, but the worst of it was over. One more muffled blast beneath the crumpled hood and you could kiss the German engine off.

He turned away and put the high-tech funeral pyre behind him, moving toward his rental car. Three soldiers, give or take, would make no lasting difference to Sylvester Ramos, but the message would be driven home.

Again.

By now the dealer's paranoia would be mounting as he cast about for enemies with hardware, nerve and brains enough to make this kind of challenge in the face of overwhelming might. And if he came up empty, that was fine. Another cause for indecision, bleeding into panic as the day went on.

No doubt about it—things were looking bad for Ramos at the moment.

And the dealer's luck was just about to go from bad to worse.

9

"We're clean," Sergeant Robert Grissom said, completing his third aimless circuit of Kate Sessions Park. "No tail."

"Okay," Lassiter replied, "let's get it done."

The unmarked cruiser rolled south on Lamont to Garnet Avenue, eastbound from there to Olney, with another jog south to Grand. Despite an unaccustomed case of nerves, Lassiter didn't believe that anyone could follow them this far without a slipup, something to betray the fact that they were being shadowed.

There was still a possibility of bugs inside the car, of course, but that was stretching it. They kept their conversation to a minimum, in any case, Lassiter feeling tense and uncommunicative as they neared the rendezvous.

De Anza Cove lay due south of the Mission Bay golf course, boasting luxury condos, a popular beach and boats available for hire. It was well off Lassiter's normal range, with a lieutenant's salary from the sheriff's department, but that made it less likely the two of them would be observed when they kept their appointment. Less likely, still, that they'd drive into the middle of an ambush, getting caught up in the recent shitstorm that was blowing up in San Diego.

"Was he pissed, or what?" Grissom asked, covering the last two blocks before they reached the meeting site.

"More curious, I'd say. Of course, I didn't tell him anything to speak of on the phone."

"I still think we could handle this all right ourselves."

"You're on the record, Bob. If I want something done, I'll let you know."

"Your call."

"That's right, it is."

He felt the angry waves radiating from the driver's seat and let it go. To hell with Grissom, if he couldn't take instructions like the others. Hammering away at his complaints once a decision had been made was foolish, a display of weakness. Lassiter had tried to get that point across on more than one occasion, but the sergeant wasn't quick to take a hint.

If he persisted, Lassiter might have to use a more persuasive form of argument.

They found a parking place, their cruiser facing toward the water, bathing suits and young tanned bodies splashing through the surf. No bikers or assorted human trash on this beach, with the high-priced condos staring down behind him. Trolls and garbage pickers were discouraged by strict application of trespassing statutes, arrests and citations amounting to harassment, but it did the trick. The well-to-do could splash and sun themselves in relative serenity, without some burned-out bag lady breathing down their necks, begging for change.

Strictly speaking, it wasn't a private beach, but theory and practice were worlds apart in San Diego, as in every other major city coast to coast. It might be a free country on paper, but exclusive areas were keeping up their guard against the rising tide of riffraff, less concerned with housing and feeding the homeless than with sweeping them out of sight. Teenagers still raised hell along the beach from time to time, but they were all from "better" homes, and thus excused by divine right.

"Here goes."

Lassiter checked his right-hand mirror, picking out the Lincoln as it came around behind him, blocking their retreat, the engine idling in perfect tune.

"You stick, but give him room."

"Like always."

Lassiter walked back to the Lincoln and found the driver waiting for him with the back door open, waiting. Inside, the air conditioner was going full-blast, circulating a cloud of expensive cologne.

"You're looking healthy, Darren," Ramos commented as they began to move.

"I feel okay."

"You didn't sound it on the phone."

"Well, like I told you, there's a problem."

"So?"

He spelled it out for Ramos, leaving out Louisa's name at first but running down the basics of her story, all that shit about a living witness and the rumors of Sylvester putting out a contract on the wets. He knew enough to meet the dealer's gaze as he explained, and he could see the dark eyes smoldering before he finished.

"This sergeant . . . what's his name again?"

"I'd rather not get into that unless it's absolutely necessary."

"I decide what's necessary, Darren. Let me have the name."

"Louisa Escobar."

"A woman?"

"Don't get stuck on that. She's plenty sharp, I guarantee."

"You say so, Darren. But she doesn't have a name? No leads on who this so-called witness is or where he can be found?"

"Not yet."

"I really don't see any problem, then."

"I told you—"

"Rumors, Darren. So she hears I gave the order. That's no kind of evidence."

"It makes her want to keep on digging, though."

"You're still the boss, amigo, am I right? You tell her where to dig and what to leave alone?"

"She's got the case," Lassiter said, defensive now. "I can't just order her to let it slide."

"Okay, I hear you. Let's say she keeps digging. Her reports come back to you?"

"That's right."

"And you decide what action must be taken, no?"

"That's how it works."

"So what's the fucking problem, Darren?"

"If she digs up something solid and I try to shine it on, I can't predict how she'll react. An end run maybe. She could go over my head if she thinks I'm stonewalling."

"We can't let that happen, amigo. You have as much to lose on this as I do. Maybe more."

"I know that, damn it!"

"So we're in agreement, then. You'll keep an eye on this Louisa Escobar and stop her if she rocks the boat. Can do?"

"I haven't let you down so far."

"That's right. You've got a perfect record, Darren. Try to keep it that way, hmm?"

"I'll see what I can do."

A nod from Ramos, and his driver curbed the Lincoln, sitting still this time while Lassiter crawled out. He watched the limo disappear in traffic, feeling vaguely nauseated while he waited for the unmarked squad to pick him up.

A perfect record, right.

And if he wanted it to stay that way, he just might have to kill a fellow cop.

THE CALL CAME THROUGH at 1:15 p.m., and Johnny caught it on the second ring. "Hello?"

"Are we secure?" his brother asked.

"Hang on a sec. I'll put it on the box."

When they were duly scrambled, Johnny said, "You've had a busy day so far."

"I'm warming up. How did it go with the authorities?"

"About like we expected. I touched base with the sergeant in charge of the case, dropped some hints, but she wasn't convinced."

"You mentioned Ramos?"

"And the witness. She was skeptical on both ends."

"If there is a witness, we should try to get in touch."

"That's easy said. They almost had to beat it back to Mexico, and that was going on five days ago. They could be anywhere by now."

"A border crossing won't be a problem."

"If you're going south, I'd like to tag along."

"They also serve—"

"Who only stand and wait, I know. Let's say I'm tired of serving. Did you ever stop and think that this is *my* gig?"

"Fair enough. I've got a few more stops to make before we leave. What say I call you back in, oh, two hours, and we go from there?"

"You wouldn't try to put one over on me, would you?"

Bolan chuckled softly on the other end. "You want to see the sights, somebody has to keep you out of trouble, little brother."

"Thanks a heap."

"Don't mention it. I'll be in touch."

The line went dead, and Johnny switched off the scrambler. The Strongbase line, with all its cutouts, should have been secure, but you could never be too careful. Mack was carrying a miniscrambler that was readily attached to any telephone, and they could keep in touch that way without the fear of taps or random pick-ups on the line.

A few more stops to make.

He knew what that meant in his brother's terms, and Johnny knew he'd spend the next two hours worrying despite himself. It was a futile exercise, of course, and he resented it to some extent when anybody made protective moves on him, but he couldn't deny his feelings where his brother was concerned.

From age twelve Johnny had been getting used to the idea of Mack as a statistic, killed in action. First in Vietnam when every evening brought the war into his living room, and then at home when Mack was taking on the Mafia in what appeared to be a hopeless one-man war. His brother's death had even been announced on one occasion in New York, but Johnny had missed the funeral, and his adoptive parents had worried—with sufficient reason—that the Mob would have spotters in attendance, watching out for any stray survivors of the Bolan clan.

Later, when Mack was "reborn" as Colonel John Phoenix, Johnny had begun to think that anything was possible. And yet he knew his brother was no Superman, no automated Terminator who could take a hundred mortal hits and still keep rolling. Flesh and blood could only stand so much or last so long. One day...

He blanked the morbid thoughts out of his mind and concentrated on the hours ahead. If they were going south together, he had preparations to complete. They'd be needing hardware, light and portable without sacrificing stopping power; wheels to get them there and back again; perhaps some cash to spread around if they were called upon to pay for leads.

It still might be a wasted effort, but he didn't think so. Facing combat in the military, later living on the edge with Mack, he had learned to trust his instincts. Call them hunches or whatever, Johnny's gut impressions had saved his life on more than one occasion, and the gut was talking to him now.

A witness.

Someone who could help fill in the blanks and put it all together.

Waiting.

Mexico was still no more than sixty-forty in the way of probabilities, but it would be a place to start. And if they came up empty on the witness, there were targets worthy of attention in the neighborhood. Whichever way it went, he had a feeling that the trip wouldn't be wasted.

Johnny only hoped that it wouldn't turn out to be a one-way journey for his brother and himself.

He had no wish to die in Mexico, but "where" was less important in the final scheme of things than "how" and "why."

Whatever might be waiting for them in the streets of Tijuana or beyond, the Bolan brothers would meet it head-on, no quarter asked or offered.

And when the smoke cleared, they'd find out who was still alive.

THE TRUCKING BUSINESS WAS a minor sideline for Sylvester Ramos, useful as a means of transportation for illegal shipments now and then, more often as a cover for the income Ramos opted to report for taxes. On the surface everything looked spotless, but the operation kept a double set of books, and no one but the manager—a lowlife named Albert Torres—and a couple of supporting hardmen was privy to the Ramos link.

The combination warehouse and garage off Fletcher Parkway in the heart of El Cajón had three rigs in the lot when Bolan pulled his rental in and parked beside the loading dock. He had a photocopy of the manager's mug shot to work with as he left the car, an Ingram MAC-10 and a canvas satchel going with him as he mounted concrete stairs.

"Can I help you?" someone asked behind him.

Bolan turned to find a driver gaping at his hardware, looking as if he didn't know if he should run or simply faint.

"Why don't you help yourself?" the Executioner suggested. "Take a hike."

"I'm gone."

He didn't even use the stairs, opting for a six-foot drop and disappearing at a run while Bolan watched him go.

One down.

The interior of the warehouse was cool and quiet. Bolan followed muffled voices to a makeshift office, walls of fiberglass and plywood with an open doorway. Three men huddled in a ring around the central desk.

He made the manager at once and pegged the other two as shooters, sport coats covering their weapons while the man in charge had left his hanging on a wall hook. Bolan filled the doorway, giving them time to notice him before he spoke. "I hate to interrupt."

The shooters saw his weapon but tried it, anyway, despite the odds. One broke away to Bolan's right, the other to his left, as if it mattered. Given more space and some decent cover, it would probably have worked, but they were standing in an open box, no more than ten feet square.

He nailed the runner on his left, a 3-round burst across the chest that bounced him off a filing cabinet and dumped him facedown on the concrete floor. On Bolan's right the second hardman had one hand inside his jacket, hauling on a shoulder rig, but he'd never have a chance to draw. The second burst from Bolan's Ingram punched him over backward in an awkward, boneless sprawl.

"Your turn," he told the manager.

"I got a choice?"

"We all have choices, Albert."

"Hey, do I know you?"

"*I* know *you*. That's all that counts."

"Okay, if you say so. What's the deal?"

"If you take a message back to Ramos, you can walk. This time."

"What kind of message?"

"It's an easy one. He's been too pushy lately, so he's going out of business. Got it?"

Torres blinked, his features looking pained.

"Sylvester isn't going to like that."

"So?" The Ingram rose to the level of his face.

"So nothing. I'm just telling you he ain't the kind to take this lying down."

"I'll risk it."

"Sure, okay. That's it?"

"Unless you want to try that pistol in the desk."

"Not me. You say we're done, I hit the fucking bricks."

"So hit them."

Torres scuttled past him and away without a backward glance. When he was out of sight, the Executioner slid one hand into his OD satchel, drawing out a plastic charge with a timer snugly in place. He gave himself five minutes, dropped it onto the cluttered desk and turned away.

Outside, he left another charge with each rig in the parking lot, adjacent to the fuel tanks, timers set for shorter intervals on each. There was no sign of Albert Torres as he walked back to his car, and Bolan figured the man was running as if his life depended on it... which, in fact, it did.

He sat behind the rental's wheel and waited for the timers to run down. The charges blew together more or less, with something like two seconds in between the first and fourth explosions. All three semi-rigs were totaled, and the north wall of the warehouse exploded as if punched with a giant fist. A door spun off its hinges, clattering across the asphalt, and he had a glimpse of leaping flames inside.

Whatever they were storing in the warehouse, there might still be time to save a portion of the cargo if the fire department showed up soon enough. He left them to it, rolling out of there and joining eastbound traffic on the parkway.

His adversary had to feel the pinch by now, and Ramos wasn't known for his excessive self-control. From all the evidence he was a steady counterpuncher, not above preemptive strikes if circumstances favored his success.

By now the dealer would be running down his list of enemies, attempting to decide who hated him enough—or had the guts—to take him on in open combat. His selection was of no concern to Bolan at the moment. All the Executioner required was a distraction, something that would occupy his enemy, confuse the issue while he struck a few more body blows.

He thought about the border crossing, wishing he could leave his brother out of it, but Johnny had a point. The game was his as much as Bolan's, maybe more so, and the "kid" was old enough to look out for himself. If he tried cutting Johnny out of it at this point, it would be a futile gesture and a rash disservice to them both.

Another stop or two, allowing Johnny time to gather the equipment they would need, and they could hit the road. There might not be a witness, after all, but Bolan still had targets waiting in Tijuana and environs. Either way the trip wouldn't be wasted.

10

Louisa Escobar was worried. Since her one-on-one with Lassiter, she'd been troubled by a sense of something wrong, irrevocably out of place. She couldn't put her finger on the problem—something in her supervisor's attitude perhaps—but it was eating at her, making her feel ill at ease.

She understood Lassiter's skepticism to a point, but he'd seemed unusually brusque, refusing even to consider the possibility of a surviving witness or a link between Sylvester Ramos and the desert massacre. It felt as if his mind had been made up before she had ever started speaking, a negative attitude totally at odds with the lieutenant's usual encouragement for innovation and initiative. It was almost as if he'd made up his mind that the case was hopeless, beyond solution.

She blocked the train of thought before it took her any further. Lassiter was simply doing his job and nothing more. The lieutenant was a veteran of the force with umpteen commendations in his file. She had no reason to question his motives or integrity, and yet...

He hadn't told her to forget about the lead exactly, although his manner made it clear in no uncertain terms that he believed she was wasting her time—and the department's money—in pursuit of a shadow. Still, if she could track down the witness, bring him or her to Lassiter in the flesh, alive and talking, he'd have to change his mind.

She thought about her own motives for a moment, trying to decide if she was more interested in solving the case or proving her own hunch correct. In the final analysis it hardly mattered. If the two goals coincided, fine. And if Lassiter was right, the witness nonexistent, she'd be the first to admit her mistake.

Mexico was another kind of problem, though. She couldn't even go to Lassiter with that one, the suggestions that she slip across the border for a while and play detective on the other side. She knew the rules as well as anyone where jurisdiction was concerned. You didn't trespass into city territory without authorization or an invitation from metro police, and you *never,* under any circumstances, crossed the border without official sanction. Case closed.

The problem was that her instinct told her the witness had to be in Baja. Where else would he—or she—go after seeing fifteen others shot down in their tracks midway between the border and San Diego? Retreat was the natural reaction in such circumstances, an escape to more familiar surroundings, where you could hide among your own people.

On a less traumatic scale she knew the feeling. Going off to college, and later the sheriff's academy, had made Louisa wish that she could run and hide among her people, too. The difference was that no one had been trying to kill her.

Not then.

But if she chased this lead to its conclusion, possibly into the backyard of Sylvester Ramos, that could change. The dealer had no qualms about attacking officers he couldn't bribe, although he was smart enough to let his hardmen do the dirty work. In normal circumstances Ramos wouldn't be caught carrying a weapon, much less with blood on his hands.

So much for the problem. What Louisa needed were solutions, and she wouldn't find them at her desk, sitting around and waiting for the telephone to ring. Nor would she find them on the streets, where more and more of her informants sang the same old song.

A witness, still alive.

Perhaps in Mexico.

Okay.

If she was going, she'd have to do it right. Her shift ran out at five o'clock, and she could wait that long. Off duty she could always argue that she needed to unwind a little from the past few days, get back to her roots or whatever came to mind. If worse came to worst, at least she wouldn't be crossing the border in an official capacity, taking the job with her into alien—and sometimes hostile—territory.

But she didn't relish going into Baja on her own this time. She spoke the language and could pass for native if she had to, but her years with the department had impressed her with the need for backup in potential killing situations. Call for help before you made your move, and when the shit came down, you would be covered.

Right.

Except she couldn't call for backup, this time. Not official backup, anyway.

Who else?

She palmed the lawyer's card and studied it for several moments, wondering. No reason to believe the mouthpiece knew his ass from his elbow in terms of self-defense, but there had been an air of confidence about him she couldn't deny. A lawyer could be useful if she stumbled into trouble on the other side, and he had—or claimed to have—the extra advantage of contacts in Baja via his supposed clients. If nothing else, he was responsible for her predicament, for bringing her the story of a massacre survivor in the first place. It was only fitting that he should share some portion of the risk.

Assuming he agreed to play along, that is.

There was one way to find out, she decided, reaching for the telephone.

THE WOMEN WERE STRICTLY a sideline for Ramos, more like pretty playthings that coincidentally turned a profit. Some of them worked the streets these days, but the dealer kept his personal favorites at a party house off San Miguel in Lemon Grove. The girls were free to come and go when they weren't entertaining customers, and they enjoyed a life of relative luxury in comparison with most streetwalkers and call girls.

Until today.

The Executioner drove east on San Miguel and caught the turnoff, using Johnny's annotated city map to navigate. Two blocks from Berry Park he passed the party house and made a drive-by, circling the block to look for sentries, any indication of an ambush in the making.

Ramos would be going hard by now, but he apparently didn't consider this part of his operation threatened by the unknown enemy. If there were guards on duty at the party house, they had to be inside, perhaps relaxing in the knowledge they'd drawn an easy post.

Surprise.

He parked downrange and made a small adjustment to the extra shoulder harness as he left his car. Besides the 93-R in its armpit holster, he was carrying the stubby Ingram MAC-10 with suppressor, hanging underneath his right arm on a swivel rig. His jacket was unbuttoned, granting instant access to the weapon of his choice, but he could still pass muster as a well-dressed businessman in search of some diversion to alleviate the tension of a hectic day.

He didn't know how Ramos ran his brothel, whether customers were forced to make appointments in advance or use a special password on arrival, but he felt prepared for anything. If he was challenged at the door, all bets were off, and he'd have to blast his way inside. He didn't plan to harm the women or their paying johns, but he'd deal with armed resistance as it came. The slim incendiary sticks that filled an inside pocket of his sport coat would do the rest.

He mounted concrete steps and tried the doorbell, waiting three-quarters of a minute for a sound of footsteps on the other side. The heavy hand-carved door was opened by a stylish woman in her middle-thirties, sandy blond, curvaceous in a scoop-necked velvet dress that terminated well above her knees.

"Can I help you?"

Bolan took a gamble. "I'm not sure. Your house comes highly recommended by a friend of mine in advertising. I'm not sure if I should mention any names."

"When you say recommended, what exactly do you have in mind?"

"Some relaxation, this and that. My friend calls this his home away from home."

He read the caution in her eyes as she replied, "You wouldn't be a civil service type by any chance? Police, for instance?"

Bolan made a show of looking nervous as he fumbled for his wallet. "Not at all," he promised, showing her a driver's license in the name of Mike Belasko, with a glimpse of platinum from Amex and a Visa gold card on the side.

"In that case please come in."

Her smile had picked up several hundred candlepower in the past few seconds, and she looped her arm through Bolan's as she led him to a sunken living room. The stairs were on his left, a kitchen just beyond, the bedrooms overhead. If there were vehicles around the premises, they had to be in back.

Three girls were watching television in the living room, and all three turned to greet the new arrival as he entered, none of them at all embarrassed by the fact that they were wearing see-through negligees and nothing else.

The hostess introduced him. "Mr. Belasko, this is Rose, and Julie in the middle, Trish on the other side. If you see anything you like..."

"I'm not dead yet," he told her, smiling ruefully, "but as it is, I haven't got the time."

"Excuse me?"

Bolan drew his jacket back and let her see the Ingram. "The ladies may need something else to wear before they leave."

"Hey, what the hell is this?"

"It's closing time," he answered curtly. "If you hustle—no pun intended—I suspect you just have time to clear the place before I burn it down."

"You must be fucking nuts!" the hostess snapped.

"I've heard it said. I'm also deadly serious. You've got three minutes, starting now."

For emphasis he triggered off a 3-round burst that blew the television apart. The girls were moving now, a sight to see as they went racing for the stairs. The hostess, meanwhile, stood and glared at Bolan, mad enough to spit and scared enough to know she shouldn't press her luck.

"You know who owns this place?" she asked him when the best part of a minute had elapsed.

"It's why I'm here. Sylvester's going out of business."

"You *are* nuts."

"And you're running out of time," he told her, waggling his Ingram in the general direction of the door.

"Okay, I'm going. Jeez, I'd like to be around to watch when Ramos gets his hands on you."

"Hang out around his place the next few days, and you just might get your wish. Now move!"

The other girls were coming back downstairs, none of them fully dressed, but they were working on it, wriggling into sweaters, hopping on one foot to manage slacks. They had acquired a fourth companion while upstairs, a slender redhead wrapped up in a terry robe, her shoes in one hand, clothes across the other arm.

He stopped them halfway to the exit, asking, "Is there anybody left upstairs?"

"We're it," the chesty blonde replied. "You wanted us to leave, we're going. Right?"

"So long."

Bolan backtracked to the living room. He didn't bother checking out the upstairs rooms. A high overhand pitch, and one of his incendiaries touched down on the landing, sputtering to life with enough heat to set the carpet blazing in a few short seconds. By the time it caught he had already hit parlor, dining room and kitchen, leaving them to burn as he retreated toward fresh air.

And met two gunners coming up the walk. The women were huddled off to one side, frightened, watching.

Both men had their side arms drawn as Bolan left the house, and there was no time for discussion. The warrior let the Ingram rip, a rising, corkscrew burst that lasted something like a second and a half before the magazine ran dry. Downrange his human targets jerked and shuddered, taking hits, one flopping over onto his back, the other dropping to his knees and facing Bolan for another moment, glaring with accusatory eyes. At last the light winked out in there, and Bolan watched the gunner topple forward onto his face.

A couple of the working girls were crying now, as Bolan passed by, but he couldn't come up with any words to make it better. They were on their own, and he was on his way.

To Baja.

AT FIRST he thought the phone call would be Mack, reporting in, and he was startled when he recognized the voice of Sergeant Escobar. He thought she sounded ill at ease, without the strong self-confidence she had displayed when they were talking in her office earlier that day.

"I hope it's not an inconvenient time for me to call," she said when they had buried the amenities.

"No problem. Can I help you, Sergeant?"

"I've been checking out your story on potential witnesses, and several of my sources on the street confirm a possible survivor. I'm not sold by any means, but let's just say I think it's worth a closer look."

"Okay."

He meant to let her do the work this time, and wondered how she liked the taste of crow.

"I don't suppose you've come by any further details since we spoke?"

"Unfortunately, no. Of course, I don't have your resources, Sergeant."

She let that pass, and Johnny had a sudden hunch that she was flying solo. Curious, and yet . . .

"My sources aren't unanimous, but the majority agree this witness—if there is a witness—would be hiding out in Mexico."

"Makes sense to me."

"You understand I have no jurisdiction on the other side."

"The *federales* shouldn't mind."

"I'd rather not announce my visit," she replied.

"Your call," he said, and gave her credit for avoiding one potential trap. "If you come up with anything at all—"

"That's why I'm calling, Mr. Gray."

"Why don't we make it John?"

She let that pass and said, "I thought your clients might be helpful, if I had a chance—"

"I'm sorry," Johnny cut her off, "but they're extremely nervous of police right now. I'm sure you understand. They're adamant about not meeting anybody from the States."

"Okay, forget it."

"On the other hand," he said, "I don't mind coming with you, strictly unofficial, if you think it would help."

She thought about it for a moment before she said, "It might at that. You understand that everything we do is unofficial once we cross the line."

"Of course."

"Well, if you're sure you have the time . . ."

Was he imagining the sound of relief in her voice? He didn't think so, but he didn't know the lady well enough to ask. Not yet.

"I'll make the time," he said. "I have a few things that I have to clear up first before we go."

"Of course. I don't get off till five o'clock myself. What say I call you back at half past, and we can figure out what goes from there?"

"Suits me. Same number," Johnny told her. "I'll be waiting for your call, or checking in for messages if something ties me up. We'll touch base either way."

"Okay, till then."

She sounded better as she severed the connection, but he couldn't shake the feeling that her mind was troubled. Somewhere, in the process of examining his story, she had hit a snag. It could have been official, anything from obstinate superiors to evidence that had sold her on the notion of police involvement in the massacre. Whatever, she wasn't about to spill it on the telephone, and there was every chance she might keep it to herself when they were face-to-face.

Especially given the surprise she had in store.

When Mack called, he'd have to break the news that they had company for their excursion into Baja. It was bound to cause some ripples, more so when his brother learned the new addition wore a badge, but he would smooth it over. Somehow.

Johnny hesitated, wondering if he had made a grave mistake. Assuming that his information was correct, and some corrupt officials were involved with Ramos in the massacre, how could he be sure Louisa Escobar was clean? For all he really knew she could have been a member of the firing squad that night. Her evident uneasiness could be an act to throw him off his guard and make him concentrate on playing the protective he-man role while he was being set up for the kill.

He thought about it, then finally shook his head. If he was that mistaken in his judgment of the lady's character, then he deserved to take his lumps. She still impressed him as an honest cop, defensive when the honor of her fellow officers was challenged, troubled when she had to face the possibility of rotten apples in the barrel. If she wanted Johnny dead, she could have simply called him for another interview, arranged the meet at his place or on neutral ground and cut him down on sight.

No, he would trust his instincts this time . . . to a point. And if they let him down, if he was being set up for the kill, then he would fight with everything he had.

One point where Johnny and his brother stood at odds in terms of their philosophy was on the sanctity of dirty cops. While Johnny might agree with Mack in principle, raw logic told him dirty cops—and more particularly killer cops—were simply criminals. No more, no less. A cop who sold his badge to dealers *was* a dealer. He deserved no better than a prison cell, and if it came down to a life-or-death decision on the firing line, the younger Bolan didn't plan on dying for the off chance of a rotten apple's theoretical salvation somewhere down the line.

He understood Mack's feelings on the matter, and he'd respect those feelings given half a chance . . . but he wasn't prepared to sacrifice his brother or himself for that particular ideal.

His mind made up, he let his thoughts move on to other pressing business. Like persuading Mack that they should take a cop to Baja with them.

It would require some salesmanship, but with a little luck he just might pull it off.

Considering the details of his argument, he settled back to wait.

11

Darren Lassiter rarely drank on duty, but today he had decided to make an exception. The bourbon scorched his throat at first, but then the old familiar warmth began to spread, anxiety giving way to an artificial sense of well-being. He could understand how some weak individuals gave in to drink or drugs and tried to wipe out their problems with chemicals.

The problem was, it didn't work. The next time sobriety crept up and caught you by surprise, you found the same old problems waiting for you, often multiplied.

Still, he didn't think another shot would hurt him.

A rapping on his office door distracted Lassiter. He tucked the fifth of whiskey out of sight and slid the desk drawer shut before he said, "Come on."

The frown on Vincent Myers's face summed up their situation perfectly. "What's up?" the sergeant from narcotics asked.

"You know Louisa Escobar?"

"The Mex who works for you?"

"That's right."

Myers shrugged. "I know her when I see her. Why?"

"She's working on that business from the other night. You haven't talked to Grissom?"

"Not today."

"We've got a problem," Lassiter began, and briefly ran through his discussion with Escobar, followed by his meet with Ramos.

At his mention of a living witness to the killings Myers shook his head in solemn disbelief. "No way. I just don't buy it."

"Say you're right. It costs us nothing but some time to check it out. But if there *is* a witness . . ."

"What's the program?" Myers asked.

"I want you tailing Escobar tonight. There may be nothing to it, but we can't take any chances. Keep me posted. I'll send Harvey out to spell you later on."

"Suppose she comes up with something?"

Lassiter had thought of little else the past few hours, and he had an answer ready now. "We do whatever's necessary, Vincent. Just like always."

"Rubbing out a cop, that's heavy."

"We've been into heavy shit for quite a while in case you hadn't noticed."

"Wets and dealers, man. A day or two, it's off the news. Nobody even gives a shit. We ice a uniform—especially one who's covering this other deal—we'll fucking never hear the end of it."

"It hasn't come to that," Lassiter said.

"But if it does."

"I don't hear you suggesting an alternative. If there's a witness out there, even one chance in a million he could finger you, we have to finish cleaning house. I don't want any comebacks from the other night, you understand?"

"We should've let Sylvester do the job himself."

"It's just a little late for 'should have,' don't you think? We're in it now, and that's what matters. Now take off before you miss her leaving."

"I don't like this, man. Just so you know."

"I'll make a note," Lassiter replied. "Now move it."

When he was alone once more, the homicide lieutenant rose and moved to stand before his window. He imagined he could see Pacific Highway, Harbor Drive beyond and San Diego Bay with sailboats putting out to sea. He wished he could join them, simply sail away and put the past few days behind him. Maybe wipe the slate on two whole years and start from scratch before he had ever started dealing with Sylvester Ramos.

It was simple, looking back, to say that this or that event was the beginning of the worst mistake you ever made, but at the time he had been blinded by the glare of flashing dollar signs. He might get by on a lieutenant's pay all right, but he'd never prosper, and the pension didn't look like such hot shit when there were envelopes of tax-free cash available right now when he could use it most.

In retrospect it hadn't seemed as if he was hurting any decent people. Squeeze a stinking dealer now and then, or look the other way while Ramos did the squeezing. If some coke got through that might have otherwise been captured, it was no big deal. Rich bastards up in Hollywood had million-dollar habits, and they weren't about to go cold turkey just because some hick lieutenant from the San Diego sheriff's office had a hard-on for the so-called "drug war." Everyone was making money at the game except Darren Lassiter, and he was sick to death of being left out in the cold.

But things looked different now, damn right. And it would make a difference, just like Myers had said, if they were forced to hit Louisa Escobar. Cop killers were the lowest kind of trash aside from child molesters, but there came a time when looking out for number one took

precedence and all the old, established rules went out the
window.

Times like now, for instance.

Lassiter sat down, disgusted with himself, and poured
another drink.

ROLLING SOUTH on the Cabrillo Freeway toward the
scheduled meeting at Balboa Park, Louisa Escobar asked
herself for perhaps the hundredth time what she was getting into. Was she pissing on her pension here, and maybe
asking for a bullet in the back, or was there something to
be gained from this night's work?

A simple border crossing after work would pose no
problem in itself. Free country, after all, and she knew
other members of the force who drove down into Baja
two, three nights a week. Some spent their weekends on
the other side, if they were free from duty, dragging in on
Monday morning with a goofy, satisfied expression on
their faces.

This was different, though.

She wasn't slipping into Baja for a little R and R. She
was pursuing active information on an open case, and
that could lead to a suspension—even flat dismissal—if
they caught her at it. One thing every member of the
sheriff's team began to learn from day one at the training academy: the border was sacrosanct. Wets might
come across in droves, and smugglers had a thousand
different ways of beating customs on a crossing, but a
uniform who tried to play the game their way was asking
for a one-way ticket to the unemployment line.

At least.

The worst scenario included jail time if the *federales*
caught her playing cop on their side of the border. She
could even be locked up in the United States for certain

violations if she didn't watch her step. The sheer enormity of what she was about to do almost made Louisa turn her car around and drive back home, but she had come too far—at least in her suspicions—to drop the pursuit now.

She thought about John Gray, wondering if he could handle himself in a tough situation. He looked fit enough, but there was a world of difference between visiting a gym every week and fighting for your life in some Mexican back alley with the odds three to one against you. Legally she couldn't take a gun across the border herself, much less suggest that Gray should travel armed.

Too bad. The black Beretta 92-F would be going with her all the way, and if she had to ditch it in a hurry for the sake of customs, there was a replacement waiting back at her apartment. She had scrimped and saved to buy the second gun, and if it served her now, it would be worth the price in spades.

She felt an unexpected tingling of excitement as she neared the rendezvous. It took her by surprise, a notion that she might enjoy the dark adventure she had lined up for herself. The lawyer was a handsome man, no doubt about it, and her social life had suffered since she'd earned her sergeant's stripes, with all the extra duty she had pulled. No reason to believe John Gray had noticed her as anything beyond a badge, and yet...

Like all the personnel from homicide, she wore plain clothes. She'd changed from the conservative outfit she'd worn to work to jeans and a long-sleeved blouse, a lightweight jacket covering the pistol on her hip. She didn't look half bad, considering her mission and the worry that had plagued her all day long, but it embarrassed her to find that she was even interested in Gray's reaction to the way she looked.

Stop that!

The border run was strictly business, nothing more. If Gray was interested in anything beyond the job, he knew where he could get in touch five days a week to ask her out. The fewer personal distractions on her mind tonight, the safer she would be.

And still a portion of her mind refused to grasp the fact that she might truly be in danger. She was checking out a lead and nothing more. The witness either lived, or didn't. As far as the mechanics of retrieval, she would leave that to department brass and all the diplomats who earned their hefty paychecks for debating points of policy. Her job was to discover witnesses and evidence; what happened to the items—or the people—after that was someone else's business.

Now, if she could only make herself believe that, she would have it made.

"I'M SAYING that we should have talked it over, Johnny. Bringing in a stranger, and a badge on top of that, is worse than risky. It could blow the whole damn thing."

"She's straight," his brother answered, drumming nervous fingers on the steering wheel and watching for their contact's car. "I trust my instincts."

"Fine. Let's say you're right. An honest cop reports to her superiors unless I've got it wrong. How many people know about this little gig tonight? And how do we make sure that all of *them* are straight?"

"I'm betting that she won't report it," Johnny countered. "She was sounding edgy on the phone, uptight, as if she'd been running into stone walls all day long. I'm betting this is strictly off the record all the way."

"*We're* betting," the Executioner corrected him. "With our lives."

"You worry too much," Johnny countered, working on an unconvincing smile. "I'd say you need some rest."

"Who's got the time?"

"You're in the neighborhood," his brother said. "What say we wrap this business up and catch a little deep-sea fishing, maybe take a drive down south and meet some señoritas?"

"One trip at a time, okay?"

"You really ought to—" Johnny hesitated, checking out a year-old compact that was entering the parking lot. "She's here."

Bolan waited in the rental car while Johnny went to meet the officer. He was explaining something to her on the short walk back, a strained expression on the lady's attractive face. If Bolan's instant reading was correct, she didn't like surprise third parties any more than he did. Johnny let her into the back and closed her door, then slid behind the wheel.

"Louisa Escobar, meet Mike Belasko." Johnny winked at Bolan as he spoke. "I've told her how you help the firm from time to time on field investigations."

"Any time I get the chance," Bolan said, reaching back to shake the sergeant's hand.

"I was surprised to see an unfamiliar face," she told him frankly. "No offense."

Her tone told Bolan that she didn't really give a damn if she offended him or not. He liked that, guts to start, and he had marked the way her jacket hung, suggesting hardware on her hip. At least the lady didn't spook, and she'd come prepared.

"I hadn't planned on company myself," he said. "What is it that you do again?"

"I'm with the sheriff's office."

Bolan raised his eyebrows as he swiveled in his seat, still keeping up the act. "Excuse me?"

"This is strictly unofficial," she replied. "I'm off the clock, no more authority than either one of you, once we're across the border."

"Your superiors don't mind?"

She stared him down. "What they don't know won't hurt us."

"Ah."

He left it there, face forward as his brother put the car in motion, picking up Interstate 5 southbound toward the border. In the flow of evening traffic it would be a virtual impossibility to notice if they had a shadow.

So much for security.

"What happens if you find this guy you're looking for?" he asked, half turned in the direction of Louisa Escobar.

"It may not be a guy," she said. "In fact, for all I know we could be chasing ghosts. With any luck, if there's a witness to be found, we have a little chat. From there I have to think about reports and extradition, international diplomacy—the good stuff."

"Suppose you had a chance to bring him back?"

"I couldn't use it. One beef to the courts, and anything we got would go right out the window. Right, Counselor?"

"Depending on who raised the beef, it could."

"So I'm browsing, and that's all there is. If we come up with someone I can talk to, great. If not, at least I got a breather from the reruns on TV."

"Here comes the checkpoint," Johnny cautioned. "Everybody smile."

But it would take more than a smile, Bolan thought, for the three of them to make it through the night.

THE CALL FROM LASSITER had put Sylvester Ramos in a rotten mood. This sergeant from the sheriff's office seemed intent on butting in where she had no real business, stepping on his toes at every opportunity. The cure was simple in Sylvester's book, and he was looking forward to the chance.

Tonight.

Her run across the border was a stroke of luck. A cop outside her jurisdiction—better yet, in Mexico—was easy meat. He didn't know the names of her companions, and he didn't care. A pair of gringos, heading south to look for trouble in the teeming streets and alleys of Tijuana.

They would find it, too.

He still wasn't convinced about the witness, although he wouldn't put it past the stupid bastards Lassiter employed to miss a wet or two in the confusion, letting someone slip away and tell the tale. No problem in itself unless the witness talked to someone in authority and sparked a new investigation of the case. If someone other than his bought-and-paid-for badges caught the squeal and took it seriously, Ramos could be looking at a major problem. He couldn't expect the sheriff's officers he bribed to take the fall alone.

If it came down to that, he knew he would have to cut his losses. Wiping cops was always risky, downright bad for business, but it beat a murder trial and an appointment with the green room at San Quentin.

No, thank you.

He would ice a hundred cops if necessary to preserve his liberty and way of life. It pissed detectives off, of course, but Ramos knew there were ways to smooth things over if you played your cards right. Make it seem the cops were dirty, dabbling in things they should have left alone, and it would help to ease the heat.

Like slipping over the border to hassle Mexican dealers, for instance...or, perhaps, to make a deal. Some
money to a couple of the local *federales* Ramos knew,
and they'd tell the court that up was down and black was
white. As far as evidence, it wouldn't be a problem for
this cop and her companions to be found with coke or
grass once they were safely put away.

No sweat.

His crew was rolling, with a point man sent by Lassiter to help them spot Louisa Escobar, and Ramos knew
he should have started to relax by now. Once this woman
had been eliminated with her playmates he could take his
own sweet time pursuing any witnesses who might have
managed to escape the bloodbath four nights back.

Or better yet he could allow Lieutenant Lassiter to do
the job himself. It was the kind of thing he drew his
weekly pay to handle, after all.

So why was Ramos pacing like a jaguar in a cage and
staring at the clock? Because his family had taken three
more hits within as many hours, and he didn't have a
goddamn clue as to the source.

If he was in the middle of a shooting war, for Christ's
sake, it would help to know the fucking enemy. Without
that much at least he was a sitting target, easy prey for
anyone with guts enough to take a shot.

And someone out there had the guts.

The man was a gringo, based upon the statements of a
few survivors—women from the whorehouse and Ramón Ibarra, lying in the hospital with mangled garbage
where his knee and shoulder used to be. The doctors still
weren't sure if they could save the arm, as if Sylvester
cared.

He had himself to think of, and the empire he had built
in San Diego out of sweat and blood. His sweat, and

everybody else's blood. Then some prick waltzes in and tells him he's out of business. Ramos meant to stand and fight. It was the only way to go.

He had people on the street, all kinds of eyes and ears, but they'd yet to figure out who the opposition was. He thought of raising the reward, an even fifty grand, but reconsidered. Thirty-five was ample for the kind of tip he needed. It would shake the information loose if there was any information to be had.

And if there wasn't . . . well, in that case, he'd have to trust in luck. It hadn't let him down so far.

Not yet.

But there could always be a first time, even for the King of San Diego.

Ramos kept on pacing, waiting for the telephone to bring some good news for a change.

12

Tijuana was a different world by night...almost. The darkness and a blaze of neon helped to cover peeling paint and flaking plaster, windows that were cracked and sidewalks where the desert weeds poked through before they baked and died. You didn't even notice potholes in the road so much if you were concentrating on the crowds and lights.

It all rang hollow to Louisa Escobar this night, as on the other border crossings she'd made from time to time. She knew the way Tijuana's peasants lived from hand to mouth, dependent on the tourist dollars for survival, selling anything and everything they had—their children and their souls included—for a chance to get ahead. It was pathetic when you thought about it, desperation masked as gaiety.

Of course, it wasn't all that bad. The local cops and *federales* made out well enough on bare subsistence salaries, pocketing their bribes while they turned a blind eye to everything from petty switchblade sales to rampant prostitution, child pornography and drugs. There had been rumors on the border for the past few years that anyone with cash on hand could hire a *bruja* to perform a human sacrifice upon command, the victims cast off in the trackless Baja desert for coyotes to devour or dumped along the highway leading to the States. No one cared about one peasant, more or less, when there were dollars to be made.

If Gray or his companion understood the language, they were careful not to let it show. Accordingly Louisa took the lead once they had parked their car in a "secure" garage and hit the streets, but it was rocky going for a while. She couldn't simply wander up to total strangers, asking them about the recent massacre and any knowledge they might have of a surviving witness. First, she had to find herself a snitch—or, better yet, a string of snitches—who would play for pay.

And that meant hitting the cantinas one by one.

She had to smile at the confusion of the hostesses, confronted with a trio that included one woman. The hookers didn't know which man to proposition, so they mostly stood there looking awkward, finally escorting the peculiar group to a booth or table removed from the center of action.

That suited Louisa fine, as long as she could take the girl aside and have a private word. In several seedy dives she loitered at the bar and whispered to the bartenders, watching them palm her five-dollar bills while they nodded, blank expressions on their faces all the while. It took four stops before they scored a pair of names and general directions to the neighborhood where they could find two men with eyes and ears for sale.

Another thirty minutes were spent scouting the town somewhat off the beaten track before they met a scrawny man named Emilio. He kept the surname to himself, and that was fine. Amnesiac at first, he found his memory returning with a rush in increments of ten. When she shelled out thirty dollars from her dwindling stash, Louisa heard him say there were rumors of a witness to the massacre, but no one knew the name. Perhaps, if she inquired of Father Marcos at the Mission Santa Barbara, south of town...

Their second contact was Rogerio, again without a surname. Twenty dollars and a brooding scowl from Mike Belasko did the trick, producing information that was close enough to pass for an abbreviated version of Emilio's line.

"I guess we ought to see this Father Marcos next."

"Sounds like."

Enthusiasm didn't seem to be Belasko's strong point, but Louisa didn't mind the silent type. At least he kept his mouth shut while she grilled the locals, resisting the tendency of most gringo muscle to throw his weight around.

She made a note to check on his credentials when they made it back to San Diego. If he was, in fact, a P.I. duly licensed with the state of California, it would be no trick to pull his sheet. If not, well, she'd have to take another look at Mr. Gray himself and find out who or what he represented.

As it was, Louisa had begun to doubt the tale of clients here in Baja, looking for an angle they could use to back a civil suit. She couldn't rule it out, but something still rang hollow in the story, leading her to question Gray's veracity.

He *was* a lawyer, granted—she'd checked that far and found no black marks on his record—but the simple lack of censures or convictions didn't prove that he was straight by any means. It had occurred to her that Gray might be employed by Ramos, looking for their witness to arrange a hit, but she'd made some calls to contacts in narcotics, and he came back clean. No files, no red flags on the name... no nothing.

There had been no spare time to ask around the courthouse, run his cases down and check the sort of clients he was prone to represent. Since Gray had dropped in at her office hours earlier, events had taken over, pushing her along until she found herself in Tijuana after dark about to leave the city proper for a meeting with a priest somewhere on the highway leading south.

So be it.

She'd come this far, and she could see no point in turning back until they had an answer to the riddle one way or another.

And from that point... what?

She followed Gray and his companion back to the garage in silence. Never mind predicting futures. She'd take each moment as it came and try to do her job.

With any luck at all she just might make it home alive.

THE TRIP STRUCK Johnny as a wild-goose chase, but he admitted it was all they had so far. Two snitches off the street from different parts of town had named this Father Marcos at the Mission Santa Barbara as the man to see. Ten minutes south on Highway 10, they couldn't miss it if they tried.

Sure thing.

In practice Johnny missed the turnoff once and had to double back a hundred yards to get it right. The road was hard-packed dirt, with just a sprinkling of gravel so that it would rattle nice and loud against the undercarriage of their rental car. No lights, of course, and Johnny kept his high beams on to watch for potholes, sudden drop-offs, maybe burros standing in the middle of the track.

In fact, it was eleven minutes south of Tijuana, and another fifteen minutes bouncing over ruts and washes where the flash-flood waters came through maybe two, three times a year. The very name of Mission Santa Barbara had conjured images of grand adobe buildings, perhaps a bell tower, with white-clad villagers trooping in for mass. Guitar music in the background, coming from nowhere, the way it always seemed to do when John Wayne rode into a Mexican village at twilight.

Reality was something else, his headlights picking out a rustic fence of wooden rails, broken down in two places that Johnny could see from the road. There was no gate, and so he drove on through, parking in the dirt yard of an old church roughly twice the size of a California tract house. The church was dark, but muted lights were showing through the windows of a smaller building out in back.

"Must be the parsonage," Bolan stated, unloading on the other side.

"Let's hope so."

Johnny slipped a hand inside his jacket, covering the Smith & Wesson automatic in its shoulder sling and drawing momentary reassurance from the touch of polished steel. He had no wish to harm this Father Marcos or intimidate the man in any way, but they were far out on the small end of a shaky limb by now, and he could almost hear the chain saw growling at his back.

"Let's check it out." Louisa Escobar was moving toward the dark church as she spoke. A slight shift in direction sent her toward the smaller building, Johnny and his brother hanging close behind. They searched the shadows, wary soldiers ready for an ambush if it came.

She was about to knock a second time before she got an answer. Father Marcos was a short, thin man of sixty-odd years. His thinning hair was white with streaks of darker gray, and his clerical collar showed signs of fraying around the edges. Wire-rimmed spectacles were balanced on his crooked nose, and he was frowning apprehensively as he spoke Spanish to Louisa, clearly hesitant about inviting them inside.

Johnny understood enough Spanish to get by in restaurants, but their rapid-fire palaver defeated him. Louisa showed her San Diego badge without much effect, and her two companions showed their driver's licenses, and still the priest stood firm, shaking his head. He wouldn't yield until she dropped Sylvester Ramos's name, and even then he took another moment to decide.

When he at last invited them to enter, Johnny was expecting something on the order of a Trappist's cell, but there was comfort here, albeit managed on a shoestring budget. He saw Jesus on the wall—a portrait and a fair-size crucifix—while all the furnishings looked sturdy, possibly handmade. The living room and kitchen were combined, a single bedroom on their left, the door ajar. The tiny parsonage had no plumbing, and Johnny guessed the outhouse would be somewhere farther back.

Louisa and the padre spoke for several moments more while Bolan and Johnny occupied the sidelines, checking out the humble dwelling, each man wishing they could either find what they were looking for or get back on the road and seek it somewhere else. It wasn't the determined stare of Jesus, Johnny told himself, that raised the hackles on his neck. It was the atmosphere, a sense of prying into others' lives and maybe wreaking havoc there to further selfish ends.

At length the priest retreated to his darkened bedroom while Louisa briefly filled them in. "I think he trusts me," she began. "At least he's getting there. He'll let us see the boy, but it's a touchy business. If the kid gets pissed, we're out of here."

"What boy?" And then it hit him. "So there really is a witness?"

"Better yet," Louisa said, "he's here."

"Where here?"

"Inside the church."

The priest returned, his shiny six-cell flashlight easily the newest and most modern thing in sight. They trailed him toward a back door of the church in single file, feet crunching on the sandy earth, and they were almost there when headlights showed up on the access road.

Two cars were approaching rapidly, the second eating dust.

"I don't suppose that's anybody from the diocese," Louisa said.

"Not likely," Bolan snapped. "We'd better get inside."

The priest was suddenly confused, but he could read the consternation on their faces, and he held the back door open, waving them inside.

"Ay, Pablo."

Shuffling in the darkness, then the flashlight found a boy that Johnny made as roughly ten or twelve years old, small for his age, but looking fit enough. The kid was braced to run, but then Louisa and the padre started talking to him, taking turns. Their message didn't reassure him, but he took the bad news better than most children would have in the circumstances.

Johnny saw his brother checking out the front doors of the church, returning with a scowl. From outside came a grinding sound of tires on gravel. Someone switched the headlights off.

"We need some way to bar those doors," Bolan said, glancing from Louisa to the priest.

She asked a question, and the priest replied in what was almost certainly the negative.

"He says the doors of God's house have no locks."

THERE WAS NO CHOIR LOFT, but the small church had a stubby tower for its bell, and Bolan had Louisa send the boy up there with orders to conceal himself and not emerge until he heard a friendly voice addressing him by name. It was a desperate long shot, but the sole alternative was hiding in the padre's tiny office underneath an ancient wooden desk.

No way.

The church was short on windows, and the Executioner had no way of counting heads outside, but two cars told him there were half a dozen shooters, anyway. Of course, there might as easily be eight or ten—fifteen or twenty if the cars were limousines. Against those odds they had three side arms and some cover. The advantage of surprise was lost, their rental out in front, and Bolan had to figure they were followed from Tijuana to the mission. They had seen no trailing headlights on the highway, but the snitches they had talked to would be capable of pointing hunters in the right direction, for a price.

He spent a precious moment on the question of coincidence, dismissing it when he decided the odds were much too long. Assuming Ramos knew about the witness somehow, started searching for him to eliminate the danger, it was virtually unthinkable that his disposal team would choose this moment to arrive, precisely as the child was introduced to Bolan, Johnny and Louisa Escobar.

No way at all.

A tip-off then, and at the moment Bolan didn't even care who had blown the whistle. They were cornered, cut off from escaping in their car and damn near helpless if they tried to flee on foot. It took only one gunner at the rear to cut them down as they emerged, and Bolan had a fair idea what would happen to the boy once they were dead.

Defensive postures, then, and Bolan worked with what he had. He put Louisa in the padre's office, with a clear shot at the entrance they had used. He had no way of knowing whether she was up to combat, but the choice was coming down to do or die. At least in that position, if she froze or panicked, she'd be out of the way.

That left the sanctuary, Bolan and his brother staked out on opposing sides to bring the front doors under fire. The priest was getting frantic, rattling on in Spanish, and you didn't need a knack for languages to catch his drift. He was upset about the child, and equally about his church, a house of worship that was never meant to be a battleground. Still, they were left with no real options. It would have to serve.

Louisa took the padre to his office, but she couldn't hold him short of knocking him unconscious, and the guy was back in Bolan's face a moment later, pleading with his eyes and words that Bolan didn't understand verbatim. They had capsulized the situation, or Louisa had, but the approach of death incarnate didn't seem to carry any weight, compared to mental images of bloodshed in the sanctuary.

Bolan knew he should have seen it coming when the padre bolted, rushing toward the double doors and out into the muggy night. They heard him speaking a mile a minute, and a harsh voice answering in Spanish, silencing the priest with questions he wasn't prepared to answer.

Once again the pleading words, but this time Father Marcos wasn't talking to a friend, much less a member of his flock. The first shot sounded as loud as thunder, followed quickly by a second and a third.

"That tears it," Johnny muttered, crouching in the shadows to his brother's left, some fifteen yards away.

"It may be better if we let them in," Bolan said, almost whispering to keep his words from reaching hostile ears outside. "At least that way we have some targets and a chance to thin the herd."

"Suits me."

Their only option would be picking off the first man through the door and settling into a protracted siege. There was no food or water in the church that Bolan knew of, while their enemies were free to send a man to Tijuana for supplies. Perhaps grenades or dynamite to blast them out of hiding if their enemies got tired of marking time.

The very best that they could hope for in a siege would be civilians passing by and calling in the *federales*. That, in turn, would mean a jail cell while they waited out a Mexican investigation, and the Executioner wasn't prepared to spend his final hours in a cage.

So let them come.

The house of prayer was built for sinners to prepare themselves for their meeting with a vengeful God. From all appearances the priest had gone ahead to carry the report of other souls en route, arriving momentarily.

How many?

Whose?

The Executioner wasn't prepared to say, but if his own life ended here, he didn't mean to make the journey by himself.

He wanted company.

The more the merrier.

13

Taking out a priest meant squat to Rudy Campos. Never a religious man, he had no fear of retribution in the afterlife. Day to day was all that mattered, and Rudy always made a point of grabbing everything he could get for himself.

He'd been working for Sylvester Ramos nearly three years now along the border, but it was the first time he had ever been required to baby-sit a cop. This gringo from the San Diego sheriff's office was an asshole, you could tell just looking at him, but Sylvester passed the word along to help him out, and that was good enough for Rudy Campos. Taking orders was the way to go for now until he had enough hard cash on hand to start an operation of his own.

It made him nervous, waiting for that gringo in Tijuana, but at least he found out what they were supposed to do. Some other gringos from the States and a slick Chicana from the sheriff's office had a fix on Ramos, poking into things they should have left alone. They were looking for some kind of snitch in Tijuana, and Rudy had to head them off before they scored.

No sweat.

The gringo sheriff had a fix on Rudy's targets by the time he met them. Campos was inclined to pick them up and drive them somewhere out of town where he could waste all three and leave them in a roadside ditch, but the gringo—Myers, his name was—said they had to watch and wait, find out exactly who their enemies were looking for. It wasn't hard, one step behind them all the way, suggesting those they spoke to should recall the conversations quickly if they planned on checking out another sunrise.

Rudy was familiar with the name of Father Marcos, although he didn't know the priest by sight. He was a rustic good Samaritan who helped the peasants when he could and tried to counsel runaways without much luck. No telling what he had to do with gringos and Sylvester's problem, but the trail led out to Mission Santa Barbara, and here they were.

A rented car with California license plates was parked in front when they arrived, nobody moving in the yard. He sent two men to check the parsonage, and they'd come back empty-handed. That left one place they could check before they had to sweep the whole damn desert for their prey.

He sent Myers around back with two young hardmen to close the back door and prevent their quarry from escaping when the shit came down. The last thing he expected had been Father Marcos, coming through the double doors and calling out for them to leave the house of God in peace, for pity's sake.

As far as pity went, the padre could have talked to Rudy Campos all night long and never struck a nerve. When you grew up around Tijuana as an orphan living on the streets, you quickly realized that pity was a weakness. Every time you pitied someone else, they either stabbed you in the back or took the food out of your mouth.

So much for pity in the real world where the only law was dog eat dog, survival of the fittest.

Rudy tried negotiating with the priest, demanding information on the whereabouts of his companions first, then offering to let the old man live if he played ball. He knew it was a bust when Father Marcos started praying in his high-pitched old man's voice, so Rudy shot him. Just like that. Three rounds it took to knock the old fart down, but Rudy did the job.

Damn right.

Now all he had to do was go inside and find the others. Three for sure, plus one they'd come looking for, from San Diego. One of them would be armed at least . . . perhaps all three.

That made it tricky, but he had six men besides himself, and Myers made seven. Call it roughly two to one, and if they couldn't do the job with those odds, it was hopeless. All he needed now was someone to be first inside, check out the sanctuary and report on what he saw.

"José, Ricardo."

Rudy's soldiers didn't argue as he nodded toward the double doors, one standing partly open where the padre had emerged. They shuffled forward, moving cautiously, and slipped inside the church. José went first, Ricardo on his heels.

And now, Rudy thought, thankful for the nickel-plated automatic in his hand, we wait.

LOUISA ESCOBAR FLICKED the safety off her Beretta and thumbed the hammer back to full cock, wincing at the sound that seemed to echo through the padre's office. She had heard the shots outside, had no idea of who was firing, but she knew they were in trouble. Two cars had to mean a hit team, and the church was all they had in terms of cover. There was nowhere they could run, no cavalry to come and save the day.

She thought about the young boy in the belfry. Pablo. It disturbed her suddenly that they had never learned his surname. What if all of them were killed within the next few minutes and she never even knew his name?

For God's sake, stop it!

All she had to do right now was watch the simple wooden door in front of her, which opened toward the parsonage. If things went badly for the others in the sanctuary, she'd have a second door to watch as well, but there would be some warning first before it came to that.

Hunched forward in the padre's simple chair, both elbows resting on the desk, she held her automatic in a firm two-handed grip. The range was no more than a dozen feet, and it should be impossible to miss. Of course, the same would go for her opponents if they came in shooting. It was hard to miss a sitting duck.

Except this duck had cover, of a sort, and wasn't just sitting.

She was primed for fighting back.

The church was dark, but she'd grown accustomed to it. When the shooters came in—if they came—she'd be sighting on the open doorway, possibly a human silhouette, life-size. Fifteen rounds were in the magazine and one up the spout, with two spare magazines riding her belt in leather pouches.

Ready.

Even so the scuffling sound of footsteps took her by surprise short moments later. Two men, anyway, and maybe more. She felt cold beads of perspiration on her forehead, but she didn't have the time to wipe them off as someone started opening the outside door.

She waited, squinting over the Beretta's sights until she had a perfect target: tall, broad-shouldered, close-cropped hair. A glint of moonlight on the pistol in his hand. He stepped across the threshold, and she gave him three rounds in rapid-fire along the midline of his body, crotch to sternum. Stunning impact drove him backward, through the open door, and dropped him in the dusty yard.

One down.

Number two cut loose with automatic fire a heartbeat later, just his hand and a subgun that could have been a mini-Uzi poked around the door frame, squeezing off a burst that filled the office with adobe dust. A second burst pinned her down. She was on her knees, taking full advantage of the wooden desk, the chair pushed backward and away.

They had a simple choice of rushing her behind suppressing fire, or hanging back to wait her out. Unless, of course, they had explosives, gasoline, some other way to make her sniper's nest untenable. Police would have the tear gas out by now, but that was only used if you intended taking somebody alive. In killing situations you could pull out all the stops.

Like now.

A shotgun blast ripped through the doorway, quickly followed by another, and the automatic weapon sprayed another burst from wall to wall. Louisa held her fire, allowing them to wonder whether she was hit or simply waiting for an unobstructed shot. If they were coming in, it wouldn't hurt to have them nervous, maybe even clumsy in their haste.

She heard them coming with a scrape of boots on sand and gravel, followed instantly by a barrage of aimless fire. Instead of popping up above the desk, Louisa wriggled to her left and poked her head around the side, the snout of her Beretta locking onto one assailant's groin.

She shot him twice at close to point-blank range, and the gunner pitched over backward, firing toward the ceiling with his little stuttergun. There was a moment, give or take, when his companion was confused, disoriented, and she followed up on her advantage, lurching to her knees and pumping half a dozen rounds in the direction of a hulking shadow.

The shotgun's muzzle-flash was blinding, and she felt the buckshot strike a corner of the desk, exploding through the wood, a top drawer flying open, tattered papers drifting in the air like snowflakes. Two more rounds from her Beretta, and the hulk went down, a wheezing rattle in his throat the only sound besides a clatter of his weapon on the floor.

She was on her feet before she saw and heard the second gunner moving, sitting up. One hand was pressed against his lower abdomen to stop the flow of blood, and he was cursing her in gutter Spanish as he strained to reach the fallen weapon, lying just beyond his grasp.

Louisa put her last two bullets in the wounded gunner's chest and dropped the empty magazine, reloading as she crouched behind the shattered desk again.

To watch and wait.

THE MORE HE THOUGHT about their plan—to let the gunners in and nail them all at once—the more it seemed to Johnny like a bad idea. The waiting bothered him, of course, but mostly it was the uncertainty of numbers that had the younger Bolan's nerves on edge. For all he knew there could be ten or fifteen guns outside, more vehicles en route.

He caught himself and took a deep breath, willing himself to relax.

The numbers didn't matter anymore. Whatever happened in the next few moments, there was no way out except across the bodies of his enemies. If they couldn't escape, at least they had a chance to maul their adversaries, let the bastards know they'd been in a fight. And when the gunners got together over drinks tomorrow or the next day, boasting of their great achievement, there would be some empty stools along the bar.

First blood went to their opponents, with the death of Father Marcos, and it showed that they meant business. No survivors, no witnesses. The way they should have managed it the first time.

Johnny flinched at the sudden explosion of gunfire behind him, coming from the padre's office. First a pistol, followed by a burst of automatic fire and shotgun blasts.

"They're in," he told his brother.

"Trying, anyway. Look sharp."

One of the tall front doors was standing open, left that way when Father Marcos took his final walk, and now a silhouette slipped through the opening, immediately followed by a second and a third. His eyes were more or less adjusted to the darkness now, and Johnny picked out a target, the Smith & Wesson tracking, but he held his fire. Mack wanted all of them inside, if he could manage it, to shave the odds of reinforcements waiting in the yard.

Okay.

He counted four, then five, and then no more. He spent a moment waiting and saw no further movement in the doorway, telling him that everybody was inside, or else the team was bent on holding gunners in reserve.

The padre's office was silent. The encounter there had finished off the same way it began, with pistol shots, and that could be a hopeful sign. Or so he told himself, aware he'd have to watch his back, as well, once they engaged the enemy.

"Ay, gringos. You can hear me, no? Is too bad about the priest, you know? He doesn't help us. That's okay for you, though. *You* can help us, and we let you go, okay?"

"Help this!" Johnny shouted, squeezing off a 3-round burst on automatic from his pistol. Near the open door one of the gunners staggered, slumping back against the wall, his slide continuing until his buttocks hit the floor.

All hell broke loose inside the sanctuary—pistols, automatic weapons and another shotgun battering the air with a cacophony of death. The pew on Johnny's left exploded from a charge of buckshot, and he knew his first two rounds were wasted as he flinched off-target, ducking back to save his eyes from flying splinters.

Muzzle-flashes lit the darkness with a dazzling strobe effect, and they were all he had to sight on now, his enemies in motion, dodging in and out of cover as they fired. There were two on his right, dueling with Mack, and Johnny fired a hot 10 mm round in the direction of the closest one before he swung to face the two on his side of the room.

One of the gunners came up blasting with a submachine gun, firing low at first and wasting precious ammo on the nearest pews, correcting swiftly when he saw his error. Bullets rattled over Johnny's head, but they were high now, giving him the time he needed for a rapid double-punch at twenty feet.

Downrange the gunner melted, triggering a last burst into empty air before he fell. His sidekick had a pair of heavy automatics, firing both of them at once like some-

thing from a western movie, edging toward the open door
and covering his own retreat.

Johnny winged him with a lucky shot and saw the
gunner stagger, dropping one of his weapons, firing back
with the other. His target stooped to retrieve the fallen
pistol, nearly losing balance as he did so, giving Johnny
time to aim. When his assailant came up firing, Johnny
was prepared, the Smith & Wesson belting out three
rounds in rapid-fire.

He saw his target toppling backward, heard the strangled cry of pain. Then a burst of automatic fire ripped
through the pew in front of him, a near-miss whistling
past his cheek. Too late he got a round off at the sprinting figure, driven under cover by another burst that
nearly took his head off.

Rolling, he came up a few yards down from the firing
line in time to see the tall door swinging on its hinges,
darkness on the other side. His brother was up and running toward the exit, squeezing off a shot at someone on
the floor before he reached the threshold, hesitating long
enough to say across his shoulder, "We can't let him get
away."

And he was gone.

BOLAN KNEW THE ODDS of running into trouble in the
yard, but it would be more dangerous by far to let survivors from the hit team slip away. If they were canceled
here and now, it left their master in a quandary, still un-
clear on who—or what—was facing him. Conversely any
kind of battlefield intelligence Sylvester Ramos might
receive would jeopardize the next move Bolan made, and
he wasn't prepared to take that chance.

He took the open doorway in a rush and leaped across
the prostrate form of Father Marcos, diving to the

ground as a burst of automatic stitched holes across the door and adobe wall behind him. Close, but no cigar.

He triggered two quick rounds, no hits, and the Beretta's slide locked open. Cursing, Bolan ditched the empty magazine and rammed another home, releasing the slide lock, chambering a Parabellum cartridge even as he scuttled to his left. A short burst from his adversary's submachine gun kicked up dust and sand in Bolan's face.

Three cars stood in front of him, the rental and a matching pair of Caddies, midnight black and covered with a layer of grit from traveling on unpaved desert roads. His target was between the rental and the nearest Cadillac, a slouching shadow, cradling the automatic weapon like a babe in arms.

He moved before the muzzle-flash erupted, heading toward the rental car on his knees and elbows, effectively concealed from where his adversary stood. A short burst raked the driver's side, exploding safety glass and drilling sheet metal before the gunner took to his heels.

Bolan rose to a crouch, risked a glance across the rental's hood and saw his adversary sprinting for the second Cadillac in line. He tried a shot and missed, the gunner swiveling around and firing wild, the rental's windshield taking most of it. He ducked and came up in time to hear an engine racing.

One chance remained to stop him now, and it demanded that the warrior show himself, regardless of the risk. He made his choice and followed through with pumping strides, both hands on the Beretta for a steady grip, his eyes wide open, firing on the run.

The driver's face seemed pale by moonlight, blanched by sudden fear. His automatic weapon nosed across the windowsill, a bright spark from the muzzle, and the

Executioner kept right on firing, 3-round bursts on automatic, throwing everything he had. He never knew which burst struck home, but suddenly he saw the Caddy drifting, losing its momentum, rolling slowly toward the open desert with a dead man at the wheel.

All done.

A noise behind him brought the Executioner around to face his brother, with Louisa Escobar on his heels. The boy named Pablo stood beside her, clinging to her hand.

"I guess we're finished here," Bolan said.

"Are we going back in that?" his brother asked, examining the bullet-punctured rental with a jaundiced eye.

Bolan checked the other Caddy, finding keys in the ignition, leather seats with room to spare. "What say we go in style?"

14

It was a long ride back to San Diego for Louisa Escobar. Ironically the border crossing was the least of it, no problem in their stolen Cadillac. They caught a lazy customs officer who waved them through without a second look, Louisa riding in the back with Pablo and prepared to claim him as her son if they were stopped.

By that time she had coaxed a last name out of him—Aldrete—and the boy had told his story of the massacre in halting phrases, ending with his mother's death and his retreat to Baja, hiding out with Father Marcos at the Mission Santa Barbara. The priest had been a family friend, and he'd offered Pablo sanctuary at the church. It was a mystery, exactly, how the story of a massacre survivor had leaked out. Perhaps the padre's cleaning woman, or the local peasants he employed as handymen around the church from time to time.

No matter now. The damage had been done, and they'd have to take for granted that the shooters had communicated any information they received to their employers prior to closing in for the kill. That meant Sylvester Ramos would be waiting for an update, and the loss of seven men would barely slow him down.

Eight men, Louisa thought, including Vincent Myers.

She knew the narco officer by sight and reputation. He had twelve or thirteen years with the department, an

outstanding record of arrests...and she'd killed him
coming through the back door of the Mission Santa
Barbara with a pistol in his hand. Whatever else tran-
spired this night, she had already laid to rest her doubts
about police collusion with the Ramos syndicate.

If Myers was on the pad, prepared to kill for Ramos in
Tijuana, it supported Pablo's tale of murderers in uniform. The boy had looked at Myers before they had left
the mission, showing no recognition of the prostrate body
in civilian clothes, but he had explained that he'd seen no
faces on the night his mother had died. Tall men with
automatic weapons, dressed up like police or soldiers, he
couldn't say which.

He didn't have to any more.

Louisa explained the situation to Gray and his companion, thinking they deserved that much at least, but
neither appeared surprised. Belasko seemed to take it
hard, but there was nothing he could do to turn the thing
around. A San Diego County deputy was dead in Mexico, and that alone was bound to generate no end of heat.
If it came down to a ballistics test, the *federales* sharing
information with their sometime colleagues in the States,
they'd ultimately trace Louisa's gun. Each standard-issue
sheriff's weapon had ballistic photographs on file to help
sort out the evidence in case of an official shooting, and
a thorough search would lead right back to her.

In which case...what?

A part of her was anxious for the showdown, eager to
expose the rotten apple she'd killed in self-defense, un-
cover his accomplices and see them brought to trial. Unfortunately things weren't that simple in the real world,
where a brother officer could try to take your life without a second thought.

In Pablo's version of the massacre there had been three assassins, all in matching uniforms. Assuming one of them was Vincent Myers, that still left two at large, and there was no good reason for assuming there were *only* two. If Ramos had corrupted three men on the force, then why not six or seven, ten or twelve? How many men with guns and badges would be looking for her now to silence her and Pablo while they still had time?

If she admitted killing Myers, regardless of the provocation, it would mean exposure of her trip to Mexico without authority to carry out a search for evidence on foreign soil. Assuming she was finally exonerated for the killing, she could still be fired for unprofessional behavior, even prosecuted by the Mexican authorities on weapons charges, usurpation of authority, and God knows what else. Meanwhile the boy would be a stationary target, probably confined at juvey hall, an easy mark for killers he couldn't identify.

Of course, a minor glitch like that wouldn't save Pablo's life. Sylvester Ramos and his goons believed in making sure, and they had reputations to protect. If they allowed a witness to survive, especially now that he'd cost them soldiers in the field, it would be treated as a sign of weakness by the competition. Ramos would be labeled a *pendejo,* a person who lacked the balls to finish what he'd started.

It was the kind of publicity a dealer didn't need, and Louisa knew that Ramos would do everything within his power to preserve his macho image on the streets.

Which meant that she and Pablo would be marked to die.

It was decided by the time they reached the drop-off point that Pablo would accompany Louisa home and spend a night or two in her protective care. By that time

Belasko seemed convinced the situation would resolve itself, a confidence Louisa didn't share. Still, there was something about the child that brought out her maternal instincts, and the suggestion of where he should hide was her own.

The one surprise since leaving Baja lay in store as Mike Belasko parked their stolen Caddy in the public lot, three spaces from Louisa's car. John Gray got out when she did, pausing long enough to speak with his companion, and he trailed her to the waiting compact.

"Can I drive you home?" he asked.

"I know the way," she said.

"You might not be the only one."

"Oh, right."

There seemed no point in arguing, and she let him take the wheel. It took another moment to decide exactly how she felt, but finally she worked it out.

Relieved.

THE DEATH OF A POLICEMAN changed things, but the Executioner had come too far to pull out of the operation now. He was committed to the game, but he'd have to watch his step. From this point on the ground would be especially treacherous.

It could go several different ways from here, of course. Sylvester Ramos could arrange to have the bodies from the Mission Santa Barbara disappear without a trace to save himself embarrassment, in which case they'd simply have a missing cop. The discovery of Vincent Myers in Baja, with a murdered priest and seven gunmen, would inevitably raise some questions for the sheriff's office and the Ramos syndicate. If Ramos got the *federales* to cooperate, they could perhaps concoct some fairy tale to cover all the evidence, but it wouldn't survive intensive scrutiny.

So far Bolan figured his team was ahead of the game. They had survived their first encounter with the enemy—or second, if he counted Johnny's brush with death three days ago—and they had actually retrieved the witness they were looking for. It wouldn't be a simple thing to use his evidence, considering the risks and built-in complications of working with an underage illegal alien to prosecute police. Approaching the authorities was problem number one, and Bolan understood that he'd have to try an end run, cutting out the locals altogether, since he had no way of knowing who to trust.

The Feds, then.

The warrior found a public phone booth at a service station on Park Boulevard, parked his rental so that it would help to screen the booth and slipped inside. He used a credit card supplied by Stony Man in one of several names he favored on the road. The bills were covered—buried, really—in a secret action fund at Justice. If anyone went looking, it would take them months to track the billing down, and there would be no records of a Michael Belasko on the Justice roster when they got it done. A glitch perhaps. Untraceable. Case closed.

Brognola answered on the third ring, sounding gruff but wide awake. "Hello?"

"I'm on an open line," Bolan said, trusting Hal to recognize his voice.

"We're clean at this end."

"Okay. You have a fix on where I am?"

"I'm current."

"We've retrieved a witness," Bolan told Brognola, "but there's a problem."

"Oh?"

"First thing, he didn't see enough to sell the case in court. He's also wet, and we've got positive police involvement on the other side."

"How positive is that?" Brognola asked.

"One down so far. At least two others working for the heavies."

"Shit. What kind of circumstances on the one who's down?"

Bolan sketched the events at Mission Santa Barbara, leaving out the lady sergeant's name and rank. When he finished, there was momentary silence on the other end.

"I'll try to smooth this over with the *federales*," Brognola said. "There are two or three we work with semiregularly. They can keep a secret, and they don't take money from the dealers. Beyond that it sounds like you may need some help with the locals."

"Nothing obvious," Bolan replied. "I'm still assuming the infection to be limited, but we have no clear way of knowing who to trust."

"I'll ring up the Bureau and tap the data bank at the DEA. With our connections we should come up with someone safe."

"I have to follow through on this my own way," Bolan told him. "I'm committed now. There's no way it can go to court with what we have."

"Why bring the witness back, then?"

"There was no alternative."

"Okay, I'll see what I can manage unofficially. It wouldn't hurt to have a friend on standby when it comes down to the wire."

"I guess that's right."

"You're holding up? From what I hear you've had a busy day."

"It's getting busier."

"What else is new?"

"I'll try to keep in touch. If you have something urgent, there's the message line."

"Stay frosty, will you?"

"It's the only way to go."

He dropped the handset back into its cradle, slid behind the rental's steering wheel and spent a moment watching traffic on the boulevard. Sometimes, like now, he had the sense of being an outsider, staring through a pane of armored glass at people leading normal lives. Perspective varied—whether Bolan felt as if he were on the outside, looking in, or trapped inside a fishbowl, staring out—but there was little deviation in the sense of being cut off from the world at large.

His choice, whichever way it played, and there were no regrets that Bolan couldn't live with. At the moment he was more concerned about the present and the immediate future than his choices from the past. He could no more reverse the clock than he could change the nature of his enemies and make them decent, caring men.

Too late on all counts.

But they still had time with Ramos, even though that time was running short. When word got back from Baja, the dealer would be forced to take stock of his options, heat up the search for his enemy. And on the side he might have trouble with the crooked cops still on his payroll as they realized the high potential cost of doing business with the syndicate.

Okay.

The juggernaut was rolling, and Bolan couldn't have stopped it if he wanted to. In fact, deceleration was the last thing on his mind. It came down to a choice of do or die, for some at least, and Bolan didn't have to ponder such a choice for any length of time.

The pot was coming to a boil, and it was time to add some spice.

When the lid blew off, Sylvester Ramos would be standing closest to the stove.

LOUISA ESCOBAR HAD a two-bedroom house on Via Carancho in Claremont, a short hop from the Tecolote Canyon Natural Park. Johnny knew it had to have strained her budget, even on a sergeant's salary, but he refrained from making any comment. Independence was a primal urge he understood from personal experience, and Louisa had all the signs of a woman prepared to make it on her own, no strings attached.

They had stopped at a drive-through restaurant on the way back from Balboa Park, Pablo wolfing two burgers and a giant milk shake by the time they reached their destination. Strong with the resilience of youth, he was already sleeping as they pulled into the garage, rousing long enough to check his new surroundings before Louisa showed him the guest room and tucked him in bed. Johnny was waiting in the living room, admiring her choice of artwork, when she returned.

"Poor kid," Louisa said. "I can't imagine living through what he's endured the past few days. First his mother, and then tonight."

"At least he's still alive. That's something."

"Right. I guess."

He shrugged. "It beats the only known alternative."

"Some wine? I need a glass."

"Okay."

They sat together on the couch, two feet of empty space between them, facing each other. He could tell Louisa had a list of questions on her mind, and Johnny waited, letting her come around to the asking in her own way.

"I checked you out, you know."

"It makes good sense."

"The records I could find were all in order, but I swear to God you're not like any other lawyer I've had dealings with. That gun, for one thing."

"Duly licensed," Johnny told her, carefully omitting mention of the fact that he had carry permits in a dozen different names to match his range of fake ID.

"You don't just carry, though. It took some skill, the work I saw tonight."

"You didn't do so bad yourself."

"That's what I mean. I'm trained, okay? The last I heard, they didn't check you out on weapons for the bar exam. And this Belasko guy..."

"I had a tour of duty in the military," Johnny told her. "Saw some action here and there. I guess the training stuck."

"I'd say. You do this kind of thing a lot?"

"Hang out around Tijuana shooting dopers?" Johnny smiled and shook his head. "I try to keep things simple when I can."

"You blew it this time."

"So it seems." He hesitated, sipping his wine before he asked, "What happens now, with you and the department?"

"I suppose we wait and see. I'm not reporting Myers, for damn sure. They can find him on their own and try to work it out. With any luck he'll come out dirty and they won't trace the ballistics back to me."

"You made the only choice available," he told her, realizing that it sounded lame.

"I know that. Even so..."

"You've never shot a man before?"

"That's just the thing," she answered him. "I have. But it was ... different, right? I'm on patrol, the call comes in about a robbery in progress and we roll. The bad guys come out shooting, we return fire and I put one through this moron's shoulder. No big deal. I know I could have killed him just as easily, but that was business. I was on the job."

"Just like tonight."

She shook her head. "It's not the same. I killed a cop, you understand? It doesn't matter that he sold himself and went to work for Ramos. He was still a cop."

"On paper maybe. Anyone with half a brain can see he gave it up the day he started taking payoffs on the side. If the department tries to cover that, they're wrong, not you."

"I don't believe they'd even try. It's going back and facing everybody on the job, okay? No matter how they feel about what Myers did, the other officers will always look at me and wonder."

"Wonder what?"

"How I could kill another cop."

"Get past it," he advised her. "You survived. There's no shame in that."

"The jury's still out," she answered, but her lips were working on a smile. "About your friend ..."

"We more or less grew up together," Johnny replied, circling around the truth. "He does odd jobs, I guess you'd say. We help each other when we can."

"Odd jobs."

"That's it."

"Okay. I owe you both, and I'm not pressing." She paused, eyes downcast, before she asked, "Can you stay?"

"You mean here?"

She nodded, meeting his gaze again. "I've got the shakes like you wouldn't believe.

"It doesn't show."

"Inside, I mean. It would help, I think, if you could stick around a while."

"Okay."

A sudden blush suffused her cheeks. "Don't think...I mean, it isn't like... Oh, hell!"

"I'll take the couch," he told her, smiling gently.

Smiling back, she reached across and took his hand. "That won't be necessary, Counselor."

15

Lassiter was fuming by the time he reached the squad room. Nearly 3:00 a.m. and here he was, called out in the middle of the night like some goddamn rookie to clean up someone else's mess.

Except that this time Lassiter was also working on his own behalf.

The news from Mexico was bad across the board. Vince Myers was dead, along with seven of Sylvester's people. That was bad enough, but they'd missed Louisa Escobar, her witness and the two men she was riding with. The only opposition casualty, in fact, had been a priest, whose death was bound to have the frigging natives up in arms.

Goddamn it! Couldn't anybody do a simple job these days without some kind of major foul-up ruining the play?

The wake-up call had come direct from Ramos, telling Lassiter to get his ass in gear and save the situation while they still had time. He didn't bother to ask time for *what,* because he knew Sylvester's moods and understood that reason was the last thing on the dealer's mind. Ramos wanted blood, and if he couldn't have it one way, he'd find another, possibly turning on Lassiter in the process.

No thanks.

Escobar had picked her side, and she had no one but herself to blame when it went sour. He'd tried to warn her off, for Christ's sake, doing everything he could short of ordering her to forget the whole damn thing. It wasn't his fault that the woman was stubborn, chasing rumors down until she found herself a witness in the flesh.

A witness. And for all their trouble Lassiter still had no clear idea of whether he was looking for a male or female, child or adult. He could pass Escobar's frigging witness in the corridor and never know it until a grand jury got around to handing down the indictments. And it would be too late by then for anything but bailing out and hoping he could beat the federal marshals to the border.

Shit!

A couple of detectives from the night shift greeted him in passing, both distracted by the cases on their desks, and that was fine. Officially he wasn't even here, but there was something that he had to check before he started looking for Escobar on his own. Sylvester's nearly incoherent rage had given him no leads, and Lassiter was damned if he'd start to scour San Diego with a two-man team, flying blind on the off chance that Escobar would blunder across their path.

Of course, there was the obvious. She might go home directly, and he knew they'd have to check it out. No rush on that if she was keeping up appearances. She might even make it easy and report for work tomorrow, as if nothing out of place had happened in the meantime.

But there was more at stake, damn right, than simply taking out a nosy female homicide detective. She had allies now, at least two men, and Lassiter would have to nail them both, assuming she had spilled her guts, along with all of her suspicions where Sylvester was concerned. With Myers dead—and she would certainly have recognized him if they took the time to check their kills—she'd be watching out for opposition on the job.

It was a fucking nightmare, right enough, and Lassiter would have to put it right to save himself, his job, his very life.

Time to clean the slate and start from scratch if he was going to survive.

He took his time approaching Escobar's desk, no sudden moves or furtive glances drawing more attention to himself. He sat down in her chair and spent a moment studying the items on her desktop. The telephone. A plain white coffee mug. A small glass jar with pens and pencils sticking out. The standard-issue blotter, covered with graffiti—numbers, times and dates, initials.

And the notepad.

Scooting forward, he examined the blank sheet of paper on top, then riffled through the pad in search of hidden messages. No go, unless . . .

He held the pad at an angle to the light, picked out the indentations where Escobar's steady hand had written a message. Simple, just like on the TV shows. He picked a soft-lead pencil from her stash and gently shaded in the square of paper, bringing out the message like a negative. It read: "JG, Bal Pk, 6:30."

"Bal Pk" was easy: it could only mean Balboa Park, where Escobar had met her playmates for the Baja run. The time matched up with Myers's last report. But who the hell was "JG"? Presumably one of the guys who went south with Louisa, her contact in seeking the witness.

JG.

Lassiter checked her Rolodex file and came up empty, turning to the desk drawers in a state of near-desperation.

Locked.

He felt like screaming curses, but instead he took his time, glancing around before he went to work with his pocketknife, beating the lock in seconds.

More litter in the center drawer, including several business cards. One of them advertised the services of John Gray, attorney-at-law, with a low-rent office address and a couple of phone numbers.

JG.

It was a place to start, and if he had it wrong, at least he'd be doing something, not just sitting on his ass and waiting for the sky to fall. Whichever way it played, John Gray was in for some determined cross-examination.

And when the verdict was delivered, there would be no chickenshit appeals.

SYLVESTER RAMOS had begun to wonder what, exactly, he had done to turn the gods against him. Not the Christian God, but the *orishas* of his mother's old religion who rewarded any human enterprise as long as they were pacified with offerings along the way. Of course, he didn't really buy that superstitious voodoo shit, but you could never be too careful in a cutthroat world. It couldn't hurt to kill a rooster now and then, or spend a few bucks on a jug of sacrificial wine to sprinkle in the garden, just at sunrise.

One thing, gods or not, somebody had decided it was time to give Sylvester Ramos hell. The latest coup in Baja had cost him seven men and left him with a dead cop on his hands. He didn't mind that Vincent Myers was dead, per se. The two of them had never met, and one less cop would hardly sadden Ramos, but it strained relations with his people in the sheriff's office, raising questions that were better left unasked.

A goddamn nuisance was what it was, and it could blow up in his face if he wasn't particularly careful in the way he handled things from this point on. There could be no mistakes, no further setbacks. He was hurting now, but it could still be fixed, with money and a little righteous effort. If he took a few more solid hits, however...

No.

No fucking way was anybody putting Ramos on the ropes.

He knew the rules for this game, having written most of them himself, and he wasn't about to see his empire swept away by any half-assed competition. Just as soon as Lassiter came back with something he could use...

The telephone was ringing, and his houseman brought the word a moment later. Lassiter was on the line with an urgent message. Ramos trailed his servant to the alcove where an ornate phone sat with its receiver off the hook.

"What is it?"

"Paydirt maybe. What we know is that Escobar met two jokers at the park before she headed south."

"So what?"

"I found a note with some initials. They match this lawyer's name I picked up from a business card. John Gray."

"I never heard of him."

"Me, neither. All the same."

"You got an address?"

"Only for the office. Guy's not in the book."

"We need to wrap this up," Ramos said. "It's getting too far out of hand."

"I'm on it."

"Never mind you're on it. Tell me where to find this woman."

"I'm not sure—"

"Nobody asked if you were sure, goddamn it! Are you going to give me what I need, or do I have to come and get it?"

Lassiter rattled off the address, repeating it while Ramos made a note. While he was at it Ramos got the lawyer's business address and the phone numbers from his business card, a direct line and the after-hours message service.

"I think you should take the lawyer," Ramos said at last. "If you have to mess around his office, badges come in handy."

"Right. I'll handle it."

"Is this woman coming in for work tomorrow, or what?"

"She's on the schedule," Lassiter replied. "If she calls in or something, I could let you know."

"Do that."

"Be careful, will you? We've got one dead cop already. Drop another one, the sheriff's bound to shit a brick."

"I'm not concerned about an old man's bowels," Ramos snapped. "And I didn't waste your buddy Myers. Remember whose ass is riding on the line if this blows up."

"I hear you."

"Good. Then do your part and fucking leave the rest to me."

He dropped the telephone receiver into its cradle, cutting off the homicide lieutenant's warnings. Ramos knew the risks involved with dusting cops, but he was looking at a no-choice situation. Left alone, the bitch could ruin him.

No, not while he had a soldier left, or strength to pull a trigger for himself.

But he'd have to do it right, discreetly, no flamboyant moves if he could help it. His first impulse said get it over with right now, stake out her house and crash the door if it appeared that she was home. On second thought, however, Ramos knew that stirring up a residential neighborhood and maybe showing off his guns for other witnesses wasn't the way to go. A few more hours would make no difference in the long run. He could wait for morning when Escobar rolled out for work.

And if she didn't go, then he could always change his mind, send someone out to visit her at home. No sweat. Whichever way it worked, by noon tomorrow he'd have the witness in his hands, or know where he could find the lousy, interfering bastard.

Such a simple thing to blow up in his face this way and cost so many lives. Beyond the witness and Escobar, Sylvester still had to discover who was sniping at him, get himself a name or two and then decide on a fitting punishment.

He hoped it was the Escalante brothers with their two-bit network trying any way they could to rip him off. Sylvester had been too damn tolerant of their pathetic insolence, and it was time to clean the slate. In fact, it didn't really matter whether they were at the root of his most recent trouble, or if it was traceable to someone else. The Escalantes had it coming, and he felt like killing someone—anyone—while he was on a roll.

Insurance, right. It was a good idea to cover all your bets.

The morning would be soon enough, seeing as how it was already well past midnight. Ramos didn't feel like sleeping. He might as well begin to brief his soldiers for the job at hand, impress them with a sense of urgency, the knowledge that a failure would be tantamount to suicide.

The prospect made him smile, a measure of his usual vitality returning. Time to do some real ass-kicking for a change instead of standing still and getting kicked.

The smile felt good as Ramos started giving orders to his second-in-command.

THE MAINSTAY of the Escalante brothers' operation was a warehouse out on Harbor Island, facing San Diego International across the West Basin. It was staffed around the clock by guards, if nothing else, since shipments could arrive at any hour and there was always something on the premises worth ripping off. Deliveries by sea were common while the airport's proximity allowed for shipments coming in on scheduled flights. If anything, the nearby Coast Guard station was regarded as a joke.

It was approaching 2:00 a.m. when Bolan parked his car an easy half block from the warehouse, moving through the shadows with determined strides. The bulky weapon tucked beneath his right arm was an MM-1 projectile launcher, vaguely resembling an old-fashioned Tommy gun on steroids with its 40 mm barrel and revolving cylinder for twelve hot rounds. No shoulder stock, but any recoil from the piece was covered with a pistol grip in front to keep the muzzle dead on target.

Bolan chose a mix of ammo for the strike, alternating high-explosive, tear gas, buckshot and incendiary rounds. He had two each around the cylinder, with a bandolier of extras draped across his chest. The sleek Beretta 93-R in its armpit sling would be his backup weapon if it came to that. The gas mask he was wearing gave him the appearance of a large bipedal insect on the prowl.

The warrior saw no guards outside as he crossed the nearly empty parking lot. Three cars were lined up along the loading dock, nosed in as if a speedy getaway had been the last thing on the drivers' minds. So much the better, Bolan thought, as it would slow down any gunners trying to escape.

Of course, he wouldn't mind a survivor or two as long as they were scared enough to take a message home.

From twenty feet he hit the nearest personnel door with an HE round and punched it backward into darkness. Smoke and flames erupted as Bolan crossed the threshold, scanning with his eyes, the muzzle of his weapon following. The corridor in front of him was empty, but he heard the sound of frightened voices, footsteps closing in at double time.

Okay.

Before the soldiers came in sight he triggered off a tear gas round and fogged the corridor. Proceeding at a cautious pace, he came around the corner and surprised two gunners in the middle of a coughing jag. One of them saw him coming, like a specter through the rolling clouds of gas, and raised a nickel-plated automatic in one shaky fist.

The MM-1 belched out a spray of buckshot pellets, slamming both men off their feet and spattering the walls with crimson as they fell. More voices sounded in the distance, once the echo of the shot had died away. He stepped across the prostrate, leaking bodies, careful of his footing in the blood slick, following his ears.

The warehouse proper was roughly a hundred feet in length, with wooden crates and cardboard cartons stacked in pyramidal rows. Emerging into the fluorescent lights before he even saw the enemy, he triggered an incendiary round that set the nearest stack of cartons blazing, smoke collecting near the ceiling like a bank of storm clouds.

A revolver bullet struck the corrugated metal wall behind him, and Bolan pivoted to face the source of fire. Three shooters stood in a huddle, one already lining up another shot, his buddies priming automatic weapons for supporting fire.

The next round up was high explosive, and he fired it from the hip, one gunner leaping clear before a smoky thunderclap devoured his comrades. Bolan saw one nimble adversary rolling and chased him with a tear gas round to blur his vision, closing swiftly as he swept the scene for any other hostile guns.

Four down and one in hiding when a shouted curse on Bolan's left alerted him to danger. Dropping to a crouch, he swung in that direction, picking out a gunner with an automatic rifle as the first wild rounds went rippling overhead.

The shooter would have had him with a second burst, but Bolan didn't care to wait. The MM-1 spewed buckshot in a deadly fan that dumped his adversary in a twisted heap, his rifle clattering against concrete.

And that made five, with one still breathing that the Executioner was sure of. Circling through smoke and drifting clouds of tear gas, Bolan closed the gap, advancing on the point where his assailant had gone to ground.

Five rounds remained in the launcher's cylinder, and Bolan squeezed off an incendiary from a range of thirty feet to heat things up and keep his adversary moving. Crackling flames took hold of several wooden crates that might have held refrigerators, from their size, and Bolan wondered if the Escalante brothers ever smuggled arms. It would be bitter irony right now for his incendiary rounds to touch off ammunition or explosives, blowing him away.

He came around the corner in a rush, heat baking one side of his face, and saw the gunner lurching in retreat, about to reach the far end of the open aisle. Without a moment's hesitation Bolan fired a high-explosive round, deliberately aiming high and to the right. The blast ripped through a wall of cartons, spewing shrapnel, shattered toasters, waffle irons and sundry other items in a landslide, flattening his target where the gunner stood.

He came up on the soldier's blind side, kicked the Uzi submachine gun out of reach, and used the sport coat as a handle when he dragged the guy away. There was some life remaining in the bruised and battered form, a stirring of the arms and legs as he attempted to support himself.

"One chance to live," the warrior growled, their faces almost close enough to touch. "Your call."

"Don't kill me, hey?"

"It's got a price."

"I'll pay you, man. Just name it."

"Take a message to the brothers, just the way I tell you."

"Sure, okay."

"Sylvester says they're out of business. Got it? San Diego isn't big enough for two bosses, and Ramos has the muscle on his side from city hall on down. The brothers want to live, they need to find another playground."

"Sure. I hear you."

"If it slips your mind, we'll have to have another little chat."

"No sweat. I'll tell it just the way you said."

"So split."

He waited until the gunner got into his car and drove away, then walked back to his own vehicle. So much for subtlety. If this wasn't enough to light the fuse, then he'd have to go ahead without diversions.

Either way the Executioner was on a roll.

16

It was agreed that Johnny Gray should take charge of Pablo while Louisa worked her normal shift, avoiding any deviation from her schedule in the aftermath of Myers's violent death. She routed him from bed near dawn reluctantly and shared a shower with him that was getting out of hand before she switched on the ice-cold water and curbed his ardor in a flash. Her Claremont neighborhood was barely light when Johnny and the boy departed, bound for breakfast at the all-night restaurant of Pablo's choice.

Louisa finished dressing after they were gone, taking her time and trying to sort out her thoughts on events of the past twelve hours. She had slept little through the night between bouts of lovemaking and troubled dreams that jarred her out of fitful sleep, but she wasn't fatigued really. Instead, she felt a kind of agitation that was keeping her on edge, her nerves strung as tightly as piano wire.

The shooting, first.

It wasn't simply having killed a man—three men—or even having killed a lawless cop. In any normal duty situation she was confident the shooting would have done no major damage to her psyche. She was trained for killing situations, after all, although most cops passed their whole careers without firing a shot in anger. In the pres-

ent case her natural reaction to the taking of a human life
was aggravated by the fears of what she might confront
at work. Suspension for a start—perhaps dismissal if her
border crossing with civilians was examined in detail.
Even if she sold Internal Affairs on the fact that Myers
was dirty, probably a murderer, she still faced disciplin-
ary action for violating a host of departmental regula-
tions, along with sundry state and federal statutes.

Admittedly her fears weren't confined to the reactions
of the sheriff's brass. It might be mere coincidence that
Myers and his Baja cronies had appeared at Mission
Santa Barbara twenty minutes after she and her companions had arrived, but Louisa thought the odds were
against it. More than likely there had been a tail from San
Diego, or Sylvester Ramos had his network of informants working overtime. Whichever, it was even money
that the dealer knew her name by now, especially with his
eyes in the department. So far she had only shared her
theory of a living witness with Lieutenant Lassiter, but
there were ways of picking up stray information from the
telephones, around the locker room, in office memos.
Anybody on the force who had an interest in the massacre—the shooters, for example—could have simply asked
around in Homicide and found out she was handling the
case.

She hesitated in the act of slipping on her holster,
wondering why Ramos or his gunmen hadn't come for
her already. Could it be that she was giving him too much
credit for intelligence? Was it possible that he was still
flying blind, paralleling her own investigation by coincidence or pure dumb luck?

She covered the Beretta with a stylish jacket, grabbed
her handbag off the breakfast bar and had her keys in
hand before she reached the door. Appearing normal was

the key this morning. News of Myers's death might not have reached the station yet—indeed, Johnny seemed to think there was a chance that Ramos would simply make the bodies disappear to spare himself embarrassment—but she'd have to take the game one move, one moment, at a time.

At least the shooting hadn't taken place in San Diego County, where she might be called upon to help with the investigation. That would simply be too much, a strain that would have pushed her to the edge and well beyond.

She was rolling west on Mount Acadia Boulevard, bisecting the park and angling for the junction with Interstate 5, when a black sedan came out of nowhere, charging from an unpaved access road to cut her off. She cranked the wheel around, braking hard, aware of hostile faces glaring at her from the car as she rocked forward in her seat.

She shifted into reverse, turning to scope out her backtrack just in time to see a carbon-copy vehicle nose in behind her, blocking off the street. Swarthy men with weapons drawn unloaded from both cars, surrounding her in seconds flat.

Louisa had a choice to make. She could attempt to butt her way through with the compact, taking fire from every side, or she could try to draw her gun and drop a couple of her enemies before they blew her up. The outlook wasn't rosy either way but, on the bright side, none of them was firing yet. A perfect cross fire, and their guns were silent. Waiting.

Which could only mean they wanted her alive if possible.

Another choice to make, between the unknown dangers of captivity and certain death.

She swallowed hard, made up her mind and raised her empty hands.

BREAKFAST WAS SAUSAGE and waffles, drowned in maple syrup, with coffee on the side for Johnny and a tall glass of milk for Pablo Aldrete. With something like amazement Johnny watched the boy eat, wondering where the food went in a body so slight.

Pablo seemed small for his age, but there was a stubborn resilience about him, as if he'd already seen and done more than most grown men. In some ways Johnny reckoned it was true. How many boys had watched their mothers die and then trekked miles across the desert on their own to find brief sanctuary with an aging priest?

So much death in one short life, and there was still no end in sight. It would have helped to know that giving Pablo's story to the law would do some good, but that wasn't the case. By his own admission, delivered in a combination of halting English and rapid-fire Spanish, Louisa translating the latter, Pablo Aldrete had confirmed he'd seen no faces as the gunmen had gone about their work. Before he'd slept at Louisa's house in Claremont he was shown one of her uniforms and nodded affirmation at the shoulder patch, but even that would fall apart if a defense attorney started hammering away at Pablo's age, his recent trauma, the pervasive darkness of the murder scene.

So what they had, in essence, was a witness who could finger no one for the massacre, whose testimony would be absolutely worthless in a court of law, and who was marked for death regardless. There was no way to let Ramos know he was safe from the boy, nothing to be gained by the effort, in fact. Machismo called for retribution, and negotiations with the dealer would be counterproductive, in any case.

The point was to destroy Sylvester's operation, not to help him mend his ways. And now, with Pablo in the picture, they'd have to keep the boy safe while their campaign rolled ahead.

The first step, after last night's bloodbath, was to keep their young charge safely under cover. Since Louisa couldn't easily afford to miss a day of work and thereby call attention to herself, the task of baby-sitting fell to Johnny. Driving back to Strongbase One, they made it a game, with Pablo lying on the floor behind the driver's seat, invisible to any passing motorists, while Johnny checked incessantly for tails. When he was certain they were clean, he took them to the safehouse, opened the garage by remote control and brought Pablo out of cover only when the door was safely shut behind them.

So far so good.

He had no court appearances scheduled for the day, but he'd have to notify the office that he wasn't coming in. A sudden bout of flu should do the trick, enough for two or three days if he had to stretch it out.

With any luck his brother would be wrapping up the game that afternoon or evening, possibly tomorrow morning at the latest. It wasn't Mack's way to drag a battle out if he could finish it with swift, decisive moves.

With Pablo settled in front of the television set, remote control in hand, Johnny dialed the office, recognizing the receptionist's voice when she answered.

"Clarice, it's John."

"Where are you, Mr. Gray?"

He heard the tremor in her voice and put the story of his flu on hold.

"What's wrong?"

"You've had some visitors already," she replied. "The kind with badges. From the sheriff's department, they said. Naturally they wouldn't tell me what they wanted, just that it was all routine. I told them you'd be in a little later."

"Wrong. That's why I'm calling. I've come down with something."

"Oh?" There was suspicion in her tone, but she was fair at covering.

"Some kind of flu, I think. I should be better by tomorrow, maybe next day at the latest. There was nothing urgent on my desk, as I recall."

"Unless you count your plainclothes visitors."

"If they're concerned about a case the firm is working on, you can refer them to the partners."

"This was personal, they said."

That narrowed down the field. A follow-up on Eddie Lopez possibly, and then again . . .

"Just tell them that I called in sick."

"Suppose they want to visit you at home?"

"You've got my address, right?"

"Sure thing."

His "address" was a small apartment in La Mesa, rented from the Bolan slush fund, visited at random intervals to check for break-ins and offer the appearance of sporadic occupancy. If the cops came knocking, with or without a warrant, they'd find no paper trail to Strongbase One.

When he was finished with Sylvester Ramos and they had a decent home lined up for Pablo, he'd touch base with the sheriff's office, make himself available for any legitimate purpose. In the meantime they'd simply have to wait.

He thought about Louisa, wondering if there was a connection with his early-morning callers and their Baja run. If so, the least he could do was tip her off.

He dialed the sheriff's station at the courthouse, asked for Homicide and waited for a male voice to respond.

"MacGregor, Homicide."

"You've got Sergeant Escobar on duty?"

"Not today. We got a call she wasn't coming in. Was there a message?"

"No. I'll call back later in the week."

"Okay."

The line went dead, and Johnny hung up on the dial tone. Sudden nausea swept over him in waves, a deep breath cooling it enough for him to clear his head and put his thoughts in order.

She'd been all right when Johnny left the Claremont house with Pablo shortly after sunrise. They'd both agreed that showing up for work would be the only way to go. Avoid suspicion at the office, maybe check out anyone who looked surprised to see her there. She was expecting him to call near noon, and should have left a message with his service if she changed her mind.

No message, nothing on the answering machine when Johnny double-checked.

He dialed her private number, counting twenty rings before he slammed the telephone receiver down with force enough to startle Pablo.

"Is okay?"

He forced a smile and nodded. "Sure, okay. Relax."

But it was definitely not okay. A call-in from Louisa, or from someone whose voice would pass on the phone, begging off work for the day. No answer at the house. He started sifting through the several possibilities, increasingly disturbed by each in turn.

Worst, first. She could be dead, at home or some-where else, the call a ruse to stall detectives for a while and give the shooters breathing room. A check around her house would show if anything had happened there presumably, but she was vulnerable all the way from home to work.

Perhaps a missing person. She'd fight if someone tried to grab her off the street, but there were ways to get it done. Surprise and overwhelming numbers, maybe something in the nature of a traffic accident to set her up. His mind ticked off at least a dozen ways of picking off a chosen subject.

It was easy, if you knew what you were doing. Like a veteran cop would know, or someone on the Ramos payroll.

At the moment there was only one thing he could do, and that was get in touch with Mack ASAP. The silent pager was a special model, rigged to tip the wearer off without embarrassing—or potentially lethal—bursts of noise. Then another waiting game while he beamed the signal on its way.

And it was looking like the only game in town.

THE PAGER CAUGHT Bolan between engagements, as it were, and he found a pay phone on El Cajón Boulevard, punching up the cutout number that would link him in to Strongbase One. His brother picked up on the second ring, his voice gruff with tension.

"Hello?"

"What's the rumble?"

"Louisa," Johnny told him. "She was going in to work this morning, as agreed. The squad room says she called in sick, but there's no answer at her house."

"You're thinking someone picked her up?"

"What else? There were some badges at the firm this morning, looking for me, but we haven't made connections yet."

"I'd keep it that way."

"What about Louisa?"

"No demands so far?"

"Unless they've started grilling her, they don't know who to call. I'm standing by, but there's been nothing yet."

"Okay. Are we agreed it's Ramos?"

"Has to be. If not directly, he's behind it, maybe using someone on the force."

Bolan frowned at the notion of other crooked cops involved. It was an inescapable conclusion, but he didn't relish going up against more uniforms. One of the firm, abiding guidelines in his one-man war had always been his strict refusal to use deadly force against police. He could remember punching some from time to time, maybe scaring the hell out of others with a pyrotechnic display, but he'd never killed an officer on duty or otherwise.

In fairness there had never been a case identical to this one, where the sparing of a dirty cop might cost an innocent life—another cop's, in fact. Before, when officers came gunning for the Executioner, he took it as a built-in hazard of his life-style. This time, though, aside from the explosive confrontation down in Baja, he hadn't become a target for the enemy.

So far.

"Let's take it one step at a time," he said. "You've got the boy, and they'll be reaching out for you, if they make anyone at all."

"Agreed."

The kid knew what was coming and he didn't like it, but he couldn't argue with the logic or the odds. Somebody had to mind the store and keep their witness safe, no matter what the final value of his testimony, trial-wise. Any effort to arrange a trade for Louisa Escobar could grant the Executioner an opening to strike his enemies, no matter what the heavies had in mind as a last-minute double cross. It all came down to timing, nerve, audacity.

The usual.

"Okay," he said, "sit tight. I need to stir things up some more, but I'll be checking in from time to time. If you get any ransom calls, delay the meet an hour at least to give us breathing room."

"Will do."

"And don't write off the lady yet."

"I'm cool."

"I figured."

Bolan cradled the receiver, knowing that his brother would be anything but cool right now. The hostage situation had to conjure ugly memories from Johnny's past, a past he shared with Bolan, and a love he had lost to other savages. Another place and time, but some wounds never truly healed. The pain was always there, if only lying dormant, waiting for an opportunity to surface by surprise and take you back to waking images of hell on earth.

The Executioner wasn't without such ghosts himself. He knew the private cost of waging war against the odds, when even transient victory came with a price tag attached. For every gain, each yard of ground, a soldier paid in blood, sweat and tears. It didn't always show, but it was still a fact. No fighting man on earth would tell you otherwise unless you tapped a psycho who was high on death itself.

His moves against Sylvester Ramos yesterday had all been window dressing, preludes to the main event. With the abduction of Louisa Escobar his enemy had thrown down a gauntlet, and Bolan couldn't let the challenge pass.

He had a simple recipe for dealing with intimidation, terrorism and the like: kick ass, and keep on kicking ass until the bully gave it up or died.

Beginning now.

The would-be lord of San Diego might believe he held the upper hand, but he was in for a surprise. Perspectives change like lightning in the hellgrounds, and the upper hand was often crushed and mangled in the time it took to blink an eye.

Let Ramos do his worst, as long as he was ready with the payoff when his tab came due.

The Executioner was getting ready to collect.

In blood.

17

Sylvester's secondary hardsite was a seven-acre compound in La Mesa, fronting on Mount Helix Lake. An eight-foot wall surrounded pleasant, rolling grounds, scattered trees and a house built near the water. A jetty accommodated several powerboats. It would have been a hazardous assault in any circumstances, worse by daylight, but the Executioner had something else in mind.

The Executioner's speedboat was a rental, sleek and low, providing gunners on the shoreline with a minimal target as Bolan approached the hardsite from its one open side. From eighty yards he saw a gunner on the jetty, two more standing in the shadow of the house, set back another thirty yards from the water's edge.

No problem.

Bolan brought the speedboat in to fifty yards and left the engine idling. The lookout on the wooden pier was aware of him by now, and that was fine.

He reached between his feet and raised the Marlin lever-action rifle to his shoulder, thumbing back the hammer on a live round as the big scope gave him instant target acquisition. Even as the gunner recognized his danger, Bolan stroked the trigger, sending 240 grains of death to rip the target's face away.

The warrior worked the lever, riding out the recoil, swiveling to find his new mark as a nearly headless body struck the water with a splash. It took a heartbeat for the echo of his shot to reach the other hardmen, closer to the house, but they were on alert by now, both packing submachine guns that were on the limits of effective range from where their target sat.

No point in taking chances, though.

He nailed the gunner on his left, a heart shot, pivoting to catch the third man as he broke and ran. A sniper scope was poor on moving targets, but the shooter made a beeline for the house behind him, nearly standing still from Bolan's point of view. A heavy Magnum round smashed home between his shoulder blades when he was almost to the sliding door, momentum driving him ahead and through the giant pane of glass.

Bolan retired the Marlin, hefting the MM-1 projectile launcher in its place. The bulky weapon weighed close to twenty pounds when fully loaded, but it had a range of some 130 yards, and that was more than he would need this morning. High-explosive rounds were alternated with incendiaries in the cylinder, and Bolan took his time remodeling the lake house, squeezing off all twelve charges before he took a breather to admire his handiwork.

The house was shattered, burning, thick smoke pouring from the wreckage as he braced the MM-1 across his knees. Someone was screaming in the middle of it all, a faint voice quickly silenced by the leaping flames. Bolan caught a glimpse of other figures darting through the pall of smoke, escaping while they could. One solitary gunner stood on the sidelines, a pair of binoculars raised to his eyes.

Bolan let them go, aware that frightened soldiers did more damage to a fighting team's morale than any concrete action by the enemy. Within an hour's time the story of his visit would spread among the troops, elaborated and embellished as it traveled, making one man into an army by the time it came full circle.

Satisfied, he stowed his weapons in his duffel bag and turned the rented boat for home. He felt the watcher following his progress as he pulled away, and that was also fine.

It was an easy run, no competition, and he made the dock within five minutes, give or take. The rental agent was surprised to see him back so soon.

"All done?"

"Looks like."

"It didn't take you long."

"Not this time," Bolan said. "One thing, you may be having visitors before too long. Just tell them what they want to know, and you should come out all right."

"We're talking cops?"

"Whatever." Bolan palmed a hundred-dollar bill and stuffed it into the pocket of the rental agent's shirt. "I've got a message for them when they come."

"What's that?"

"Just say I want the woman back. There's no negotiation on that point."

"The woman. No negotiation. Right."

"Stay frosty, huh?"

The agent stared at Grover Cleveland on the C-note, smiling as he said, "We aim to please."

"I DON'T KNOW WHO IT IS," Rico Escalante said, speaking to his brother through cigar smoke, "but I tell you, someone's out there kicking Ramos's ass."

"So what?" The frown on Julio's fat face emphasized his multiple chins.

"So maybe we should get a piece of that, is all I'm saying, while Sylvester has his hands full here and there."

"We owe him one, for damn sure."

"Fuckin'-ay, we owe him. I don't care what anybody says, it had to be Sylvester hitting on us yesterday. Who else you think of that would want to do us that way, coming out of nowhere like a maniac?"

"Sylvester, sure."

"Damn right, Sylvester. Thing is, we can't take it lying down. We've got ourselves a reputation to uphold. We let Sylvester take cheap shots that way, before you know it every two-bit cowboy on the street thinks he can pull the same shit, walk away with pieces of our territory."

"Fuck those guys."

"That's what I'm saying, bro'. It's time to stand up like the men we are and kick some righteous ass ourselves."

"Sylvester's got a lot of people, though," Julio cautioned.

"Tied up with all the shit's been going down," his brother said. "We make it fast enough, he won't know where it came from, right?"

"Sure, right."

"So we should get our ass in gear."

"We ought to have some kind of plan, though, don't you think?"

"A plan's good, sure."

Instead of frowning, Julio was smiling now.

"So here's what I been thinking . . ."

THE BASEMENT WAS COOL, almost clammy, with a smell of mold about it. Sitting in a pool of light that emanated from a fixture overhead, Louisa checked the darkened corners to her left and right, imagining the scrape of spiders dragging bloated bodies, scuttling rodent feet.

She couldn't move beyond a helpless wriggle in the straight-backed wooden chair she occupied. Her ankles had been fastened to the two front legs with heavy duct tape, and her hands were taped behind her back. Around her waist, like some queer safety belt, three loops of silver tape secured her to the chair. If she felt desperate enough, she might be able to tip the chair over by violently shifting her weight, but the result was far from certain, and the only thing that it would gain her was a headache when her skull impacted on the concrete floor.

At least she had her clothes, but that could change at any moment. They could cut her blouse and slacks away without disturbing any of her bonds, and then . . .

She blanked the ugly mental images and concentrated on examining her basement cell. No windows naturally, since she was underground. The stairs were somewhere behind her, leading to the ground floor overhead. A kitchen by the way it smelled, although the blindfold had prevented her from glimpsing anything before she reached the stairs and they permitted her to see.

As kidnappings go, Louisa's had been uneventful so far. No manhandling or suggestive comments in the car, once handcuffs and blindfolds were securely in place. She had contrived to check her watch before and after, but the knowledge of an eighteen-minute trip from capture to her present holding pen was little help. She knew that they were still in San Diego or its suburbs, but beyond that nothing.

Scratch that. She could figure it all by herself why she'd been abducted. There had been no questions yet, but it was obvious. Last night, before the miniwar at Mission Santa Barbara, someone had reported on her movements, possibly the prospect of a living witness to the nearly week-old massacre. She'd been snatched for questioning—they'd have simply killed her otherwise—and someone would be coming for her in his own good time.

Her mind began to cough up images of torture from the movies, television, books that she'd read. She pictured power tools and red-hot tongs, a pair of pliers cunningly applied. From working homicide she knew the kind of damage one determined person could inflict, but she was only guessing at the pain, her own ability to tough it out. She tried to plot her own experience with suffering on some objective scale but sharp reality of pain evaded her. She was aware of injuries she had survived, but the sensations had been washed away by passing time.

She'd be learning pain from scratch, then, when her captors got around to asking for a name, an address. She resolved to hold out while she could, but no one really knew their limits in advance before the test.

As if in answer to her secret thoughts, a door creaked open and she heard the sound of heavy footsteps coming down the wooden stairs. Two men at least, one shuffling while the other picked his feet up properly. She didn't turn to meet them as they circled her. It was their show, but she was still the star, and she'd act accordingly while she retained some vestige of her will.

Louisa recognized Sylvester Ramos at a glance, his face familiar from the mug books at the station house. His sidekick was a full head shorter than the dealer's five foot nine, square-built in contrast to Ramos's narrow form. The second man was studying her body, much as she imagined butchers must regard a side of beef before they start to carve.

"It's too bad," Ramos said, "that we have to meet this way."

"We didn't have to," she reminded him. "Your choice, kidnapping a detective sergeant. If I were you, I'd say my prayers."

"I do," he told her, smiling with a curious expression on his face. "The way to solve my problem was revealed to me through meditation."

"You've been catching static if you think that snatching cops will bail you out."

"No doubt I would enjoy debating this with you, but I'm running short of time."

"You got that right."

"Last night the Mission Santa Barbara. It was a fluke that you survived."

"I'm sure I don't know what you mean."

"I'm sure you do." The dealer's voice had taken on a cutting edge. "You brought a stranger with you when you crossed the border...or, perhaps you found a better place to hide him on the other side. It makes no difference. I require this stranger's name and the location where he may be found."

"Is that all?"

Ramos smiled. "A small thing, as you see."

"The only small thing I can see is you," she sneered. "If you want information, try the Yellow Pages."

"Very well. At least I tried."

Ramos nodded to his sidekick, and the man moved out of sight behind Louisa, coming back a moment later with a child's red wagon. Resting in the bed were a heavy truck battery and coiled jumper cables, their copper jaws shiny and cruel. A pair of rubber gloves lay draped across the greasy battery.

"The wonders of electricity," Ramos said, gloating. "It lights our homes, powers our vehicles...and sometimes loosens tongues."

"Is that your only battery?"

A wicked smile lit up the dealer's face. "Well said. Defiance does you credit, Sergeant. I believe I will enjoy this very much."

Another nod, and the squat man drew a switchblade from his pocket, snapped it open, advancing on Louisa with waddling strides. He deftly slit her blouse across the yoke and down the sleeves, popping the buttons as he ripped the bulk of it away in several pieces. Bra straps next, the blade warm beneath her breasts, and Louisa closed her eyes as the undergarment was pulled free, leaving a friction burn on her back, which was the least of her problems at the moment.

When she opened her eyes, Ramos's dwarf was kneeling in front of her, ready to start on the slacks. A sheen of perspiration on his round face told Louisa he was enjoying himself.

When she was naked, Ramos spent a moment scrutinizing her before he said, "Once more. A chance to spare yourself from this . . . unpleasantness."

"Fuck off."

He stiffened, angry color darkening his face.

"As you prefer. Emilio."

Waiting for the pain, Louisa closed her eyes once more and concentrated on the image of a child's face, frightened, hoping he could trust her. Then Emilio went to work, and she could only concentrate on trying not to scream.

THE PRIVATE AIRSTRIP was located southwest of town, midway between National City and Otay Reservoir. In theory it was used for private charter flights and sightseeing loops along the coast, catering to tourists and local businessmen with a need to get away from the rat race for a while. In fact, the property, facilities and planes were owned by one Sylvester Ramos, once removed by paper corporations that followed mandatory procedures and paid their taxes on time. If anyone suspected that the so-called charter runs were bringing drugs from Mexico, much less that covert flights were coming in below the screen of radar on a weekly basis, they could get themselves a warrant and check it out.

Or they could do it Bolan's way.

Three strikes behind him in the space of ninety minutes, and he figured he was on a roll. A smallish trucking company in Lemon Grove had gone out of business at 9:45 that morning, its facilities demolished by explosions from within, two pistol-packing "truckers" buried in the wreckage. One survivor, listed on the books as a diesel mechanic, had been left with a message for the hidden chairman of the board.

"I want the woman back unharmed. Right now."

The same message was left at his next stop, a small Mexican restaurant on Olive Drive in Spring Valley. The hostess tried to tell him they were closed, but Bolan's Ingram MAC-10 changed her mind. The manager was equally impressed, dismissing his legitimate employees on the spot while his pet gorilla dropped a Colt .45 beside the cash register and placed both hands atop his head. Bolan delivered his ultimatum and gave the two guys a running start before he torched Ramos's eatery. But the gorilla was too macho to let it go. He had to try the .45, against his own best interest, and the Ingram ate him up alive.

It was going on 10:35 a.m. when Bolan stopped a dealer named Miguel Hermosa. At first the man was resistant to the thought of stripping naked on a city street, but Bolan managed to persuade him with a little help from his Beretta. When the dealer's clothes and half a kilo of cocaine were burning briskly on the sidewalk, Bolan let him take a hike. Same message for Sylvester Ramos when they met again.

The woman. Safe and sound. Right now.

Time was against him, he realized, not even knowing when Louisa had been taken. Ramos and his goons could easily have finished with her by the time Johnny got word of the snatch, but Bolan wasn't prepared to write her off. Not yet.

The airstrip was surrounded by a cyclone fence with coils of razor wire on top to slow the thieves and vandals down. A chain and padlock held the double gates in place, but Bolan's rental plowed on through with only minimal resistance. The insurance would be paying for some paint and bodywork, but he resolved to leave a little something extra with the car if he had time.

Two figures bolted from the trailer that served as an office, one of them drawing a pistol from under his jacket as Bolan brought the rental to a halt. Emerging on the driver's side, he took a backward step to give himself some room, keeping the CAR-15 assault rifle out of sight.

One of the gunners shouted, "What the fuck do you think you're doing, man?"

The warrior brought up the carbine and let it answer for him, three rounds rattling off before the shooter had a chance to scope out what was happening. The 5.56 mm tumblers stitched the gunner left to right across the chest and dumped him back onto the sandy soil. Empty cartridges sprang across the hood of Bolan's rental, pattering like raindrops when they hit the ground.

The gunner's companion turned to bolt in the direction of the office, Bolan clipping him behind the knee with two quick rounds that left him bleating on the ground. Movement on the left caused the Executioner to pivot toward the hangar, where a third hardman was just disappearing from view.

Time for hide-and-seek.

The sliding doors were open wide, and the Executioner could hear an engine coughing, turning over as he neared the hangar, someone revving up a plane in preparation for takeoff.

He moved to block the doorway, firing head-on toward the little Cessna as it started to roll. Full-metal jackets at fifty feet ripped through prop blades and engine cowling, shattering the cockpit windshield and the face behind it. Bolan watched the aircraft swerve, one wingtip dipping, almost dragging bottom as it veered into the wall. Another burst found the hot spot, flames spurting along the fuel line for a heartbeat before the plane blew, taking most of the hangar with it in a rolling ball of oily flame.

He turned and stalked back toward the lone survivor. Bolan had a message to deliver, then he had to hit the road. A few more minutes and it would be time to check in with the kid.

THE CALL WAS BRIEF and to the point. He didn't recognize the voice, but there was no good reason why he should have, after all.

"Is this John Gray?"

"It is."

"A friend of yours said I should call this number, maybe talk about some trading."

"Sorry, I'm a lawyer, not a merchant."

"Sounds to me like you're some kind of a comedian. This trade I got in mind, you might be interested."

"How's that?"

"I seen the merchandise. It's pretty choice. Not too much wear and tear . . . so far."

"And what's the price?"

"Bad weather we've been having lately. Something tells me you can help out with the heat."

"Suppose you're right. I'd need to know the merchandise is still intact."

"Hang on."

Louisa's voice came on the line a moment later, sounding strange and far away.

"I'm sorry, Johnny. God, I'm sorry."

"Never mind. Are you—"

Louisa was gone as suddenly as she'd come on.

"That's all for now. She needs to save her strength, you understand? If anything goes wrong, she's going to get some exercise."

"I'll need an hour."

"Sure, why not. You got a pencil?"

"Just a memory."

"Okay by me." The voice gave out directions to a drop north of University City in Rose Canyon. "Say an hour and a half from now to give you time. You don't show up by then, we start without you."

The dial tone hummed in his ear before he dropped the handset into its cradle. All he had to do from that point on was wait for Mack to call.

And maybe pray a little.

18

The approach to Rose Canyon was easy on Genesee Avenue, checking for tails all the way and finding none. They had a new set of wheels, just in case, and all the hardware they could reasonably carry without reducing individual efficiency.

The boy had been Johnny's brainstorm, persuading the receptionist from his office to take a half day off and baby-sit at her apartment. She'd been confused and full of questions, none of which were fully answered, but she played along. If anything went wrong, she had a contact number that would field Brognola's team within an hour and let her off the hook.

Which left the Bolan brothers free to concentrate on life and death.

Mack didn't need to tell his brother that Louisa might be dead already. Granted, she'd been alive—if not precisely well—when Ramos put her on the telephone, but that was history, some forty-seven minutes gone, and there was no guarantee Sylvester would want her around for the final confrontation. Once she'd served her purpose a dead hostage was easier to handle, less trouble all around.

But there was a place for cautious optimism, even in the hellgrounds. Ramos might preserve Louisa until the moment of the showdown, just in case he needed her again. If so, they had a shot. If not, well, there was still the momentary satisfaction of revenge.

They left the car on a little-used access road, fronting the Atchison, Topeka and Santa Fe tracks. There were trees for cover, and they changed clothes standing next to the car, swapping their civvies for camou fatigues and webbing, cartridge belts and bandoliers. Aside from their individual side arms—the Smith & Wesson for Johnny, Bolan's Beretta-Desert Eagle combo—both men were packing M-16A1 assault rifles fitted with 40 mm M-203 grenade launchers under the foregrips. All things considered it was still the most firepower a grunt could hope for, going up against those killer odds. Spare magazines, hand grenades and belts of 40 mm rounds were strapped around their waists and draped across their shoulders, weighing both men down with death.

"We've got about a mile to walk from here, upstream," Johnny said. "If we stick beside the river, we should do all right."

"Your ground, you lead."

The scattered homes along Rose Canyon were elaborate, costly structures, some invisible from down below, others perching on the overhang as if deliberately defying gravity. As Bolan followed Johnny up the winding canyon, he observed that most of them had stairs etched into the rock face, granting access to the water at a whim.

With any luck at all their target would have something similar, but Bolan knew they couldn't count on Ramos leaving it unguarded. It would only take one man, and not a very decent shot at that, to hold a rugged cliff against intruders. They'd have to take advantage of surprise, if possible, and the approach by daylight further stacked the odds in favor of their enemies.

Still, there were ways and ways. If Ramos was expecting someone to come knocking on his door, the guards on his perimeter—especially on the river side—might just relax enough to make it possible.

Not easy.

Possible.

In fact, there *was* a staircase rising from the canyon to the cliff's edge when they reached their destination. No view whatsoever of the house from where they stood, and that was fine. If Bolan couldn't see the house, its occupants—at least in theory—would be similarly blind to his approach.

He took the point, with Johnny hanging back three paces, to prevent them bunching up and offering an easy target to a marksman on the cliff. So far no guards were visible, but Bolan held the Beretta 93-R ready as he climbed the rugged steps, its custom silencer the only edge he'd have for killing at a distance, quietly, without alerting reinforcements topside.

When they covered two-thirds of the distance to the top, a sentry suddenly appeared above them, staring off across the canyon first before he chanced to turn his gaze in Bolan's direction. Gaping at first, unable to believe his eyes, he tugged the Uzi off its strap and was about to cock it when the 93-R snorted twice, dispatching Parabellum manglers to close the intervening gap.

The lookout staggered, almost falling backward, but his placement near the cliff's edge made the difference as he toppled over, plummeting past Bolan, well clear of the staircase, bouncing off the rock face as he fell. A splash below them told the story of his passing, but Bolan's full attention was riveted on the skyline, waiting for the sound of an alarm or the appearance of a backup sentry on the cliff.

When neither threat was realized, he waved his brother onward, picking up the pace. "Let's do it."

AS BOLAN TOOK DOWN the isolated sentry, another pair of brothers were approaching the Rose Canyon hardsite from a different angle, following the frontage road. Four gunners occupied the car with Julio and Rico Escalante, twelve more split between the two cars trailing them at ten-yard intervals.

"Gate's up ahead," Rico said, fiddling with the safety of the Uzi submachine gun lying in his lap. He'd been playing with it all the way from home, and it was getting on Julio's nerves, although he wasn't about to say so.

Julio was too busy clutching his own riot shotgun, pudgy hands white-knuckled as he watched the road ahead.

"We sure he's even there?"

"Damn right."

And Julio had known the answer in advance. They'd been watching Ramos closely for the past twelve hours, with assistance from a pair of eyes inside the man's family. They knew exactly where he went and when, but Julio was nervous, and it had him making bonehead small talk like a frigging idiot.

With eighteen guns they ought to have a fighting chance, but you could never tell with Ramos. He was spread thin at the moment, taking hits from God knows who, not even hitting back as far as anyone could tell. If he had sixty, maybe eighty soldiers altogether, some two-thirds of them should logically be working on the streets, trying like hell to find out who their enemies were. Say twenty, twenty-five guys at the canyon house to cover Sylvester's ass.

But that was thinking logically, and you could never count on Ramos to perform like a normal human being. The man had a screw loose somewhere. You could see that in the way he ran his business, running wild around the county, fouling everybody else's nest. Some bastards couldn't hack the competition, so they had to wipe it out by force, instead of realizing that the world was big enough for everyone to share.

Not that Julio and Rico were any kind of lightweights. They could crack heads with the best of them, and they'd buried plenty of competitors themselves, but it had always been a business thing. With Ramos it was always crazy-personal, the way he had to take his macho anger out on anyone who crossed his path and looked to be getting in the way. The stories circulating on the street these past two years were like something out of the Twilight Zone, replete with torture, mutilation, ruthless massacres.

And they were going up against the man himself today. With eighteen guns.

"Right there, the gate," Rico snapped, pointing just in case the driver couldn't see it for himself.

The gates were closed, and Julio could see the guards inside. Two guys held automatic rifles, which looked like AK-47s, although he couldn't say for sure. One thing he knew for damn sure—there was no way either one of them would open up that gate.

"Drive through!" his brother shouted, clamping one hand on the driver's knee to keep his foot from lifting off the accelerator. "Right the fuck on through!"

It wasn't quite that easy, crashing through wrought iron, but they had weight behind them, and momentum. Julio was almost deafened by the crashing, grating sound of jagged metal raking down the limo's sides, and then the AKs opened up, pummeling the bodywork.

Behind them, in the back seat, Tony Salas had his Ingram poking through the gun port, firing back, the smell and racket of it filling up the car. Julio's teeth were clenched so tightly that his jaw hurt, and he found himself leaning forward, both feet braced against the carpeting as if he could somehow vicariously help their driver accelerate.

The twisted gate tore loose at last, with one hellacious twang, and they were free, running the gauntlet, their troops were coming in, both cars taking hits and giving some back in the bargain.

"All the way to the house!" Rico shouted, punching the driver's arm. "Right up the fucking steps, you hear me?"

Julio could hear just fine from where he sat, and it was scaring him to death.

DARREN LASSITER was pissed off, and he didn't give a damn who knew it. A lieutenant in the sheriff's office being called to baby-sit a fucking dealer this way made him sick, but what the hell was he supposed to do? When Ramos called, his choices narrowed down to either go or blow it off, and blowing off an order from a man like Ramos could be hazardous, to say the least.

So Lassiter was sitting in the dealer's study, listening to some paranoid bullshit while Robert Grissom and Mike Harvey sat on the sidelines, taking their cue from the lieutenant. Pathetic was what it was, but they were stuck.

There was no denying Ramos had reason to worry. In the past twenty-four hours he'd taken some solid hits, not to mention the loss of Vince Myers down in Baja, but that was the cost of doing business in a cutthroat market. The rest of Sylvester's shit, about some kid and a storefront lawyer being in on the scam, sounded like lunatic ravings to Lassiter, but he wasn't being paid for amateur psychoanalysis.

Ramos wanted him to make the bad guys go away, and so far Lassiter was batting zero.

Typical.

One thing at least. He didn't think Escobar had been lying after all she'd been through with Sylvester's finest. It was spooky, going down the basement stairs and seeing her that way, curled up on a mattress in the corner. Anyone could see that she'd been through hell, and then some. The lieutenant's stomach did a lazy barrel roll before he caught himself, remembering that he'd seen much worse with all his time on homicide.

Tough shit.

Escobar had ignored his orders—anyway, his strong suggestions—and gone dabbling in things she should have left alone. Across the border, for Christ's sake, like some kind of fucking secret agent. Never mind the jurisdiction, just go charging in regardless of the niceties. Bad enough she'd gotten Myers killed, for what he was worth, but now she had Sylvester's bowels in an uproar.

"You've run this fucking lawyer down?" Ramos asked, his dark eyes burning into Lassiter across his hardwood desk.

"Not yet."

"So what the fuck's the holdup?"

"He's an oily bastard," the lieutenant answered, shifting in his chair. "I wangled his unlisted number from Ma Bell, and we've got this little nothing apartment, nobody home. The neighbors can't remember when they saw him last—or if they ever saw him, come to that. I've got eyes on the site full-time with orders to reach out for me direct if anybody shows. So far it's stone-cold dead.''

"We got him on the phone," Ramos said. "How the hell does that work out?"

"Beats me. He may have forwarding for all I know. Unless we get inside, I couldn't say."

"His background?"

"Nothing major. He's legitimate, as far as lawyers go. That means a license, no bad marks against him with the California bar. He pulled a tour in the military, if it matters."

"He has to be tied in with all this other shit," the dealer snapped. "It won't play any other way."

"If you say so. I'm just telling you what we've uncovered, which is basically the picture of an average mouthpiece. If there's anything unusual, it's the home scene, but I need more work to pin that down."

"Forget it, Darren. He'll be here inside the hour for a little trade."

"That solves your problem, then."

"Not quite. He may have company, and even if he doesn't, I don't buy a fucking two-bit shyster hitting me the way these jokers have since yesterday. Somebody's pulling strings here, and I want to find out who the fuck it is."

"I guess that means you need this lawyer standing up and talking."

"Breathing, anyway."

"So tell your people not to waste his ass."

"Don't worry what I tell my people," Ramos countered. "What I want from you is follow-through, to clean this up when I get hold of who it is I'm fighting."

Lassiter was working on a noncommittal answer when the distant, muffled sound of gunfire reached his ears.

Ramos vaulted to his feet and ran to press his face against the window. "What is this? Somebody wants to hit me here? They're fucking crazy!"

And they weren't the only ones, Lassiter thought, already on his feet and moving toward the door. Whatever else was coming down, he didn't plan on getting trapped with Ramos in the dealer's study with a shooting war outside. His two subordinates rose automatically to follow him.

"That's right," Ramos shouted after them before the door swung shut. "Go on and earn your money for a change!"

Earn this, Lassiter thought, but he was reaching for his pistol as they moved along the hallway, wishing he was somewhere else.

"Whatever happens," he directed Harvey and Grissom, "watch your backs and keep it all together. Anything goes wrong from here, we're up the fucking creek."

BOLAN AND HIS BROTHER were advancing on the house, concealed by sculpted shrubbery, when automatic weapon fire erupted from the gate two hundred yards away. A grating crash told Bolan that the gates were coming down, but not without resistance.

"What the hell's going on?" Johnny asked.

"Sometimes it pays off, rattling different cages," Bolan said grimly.

"Whose?"

"It doesn't matter. Let's take advantage of it while we can."

Ramos's troops were rushing toward the gate and gravel drive from all around the property, at least a dozen of them visible from where the brothers knelt. A battered limo, scarred by close-range gunfire, was rolling along the driveway, two more closing up the gap behind.

One prime diversion coming up—although it would complicate their work if they got caught up in a cross fire. Doubling the hostile guns meant doubly bitter odds, but they'd have to play the cards as they were dealt.

"We need to split this up," Bolan said. "Check out the service entrance. I'm going for the patio."

"Okay."

Their paths diverged as they left cover, double-timing for the house on separate courses. Johnny's run would take him to the rear between the large garage and kitchen, while the Executioner advanced from poolside, moving toward a set of broad glass doors. His M-16A1 was cocked and locked, an HE round secure in the firing chamber of the squat M-203.

The firing at the gate had done its job, as if on cue. One of the limos was about to reach the house, still taking hits, with gunners firing back through hidden gun ports in the armored doors. As Bolan ran, he saw one of Ramos's men go down, arms flailing, but the gunners still in service failed to note the runner on their flank.

All right.

His entry to the house wouldn't be quiet, but it would be swift. Ramos's troops inside would be disoriented at the very least, and those outside already had their hands full. Anyone who tried to break off with the enemy and stop him now would stand a decent chance of being cut down in his tracks.

From twenty yards he fired the high-explosive round and watched the sliding doors disintegrate, a smoky thunderclap erupting from the room within. He followed through, his finger on the automatic rifle's trigger, poised ready to respond to hostile fire.

One body lay draped across a sofa on his left, blood soaking through a tattered sport coat. Just in front of him a spiral staircase wound away to the second floor.

He was inside for what it was worth.

Above him a gunner let loose with a shotgun, the blast of buckshot rattling over Bolan's head as he dropped facedown onto the floor.

19

Beyond his immediate objective of penetrating the house, Johnny had no clear idea of where he was going or what he should do when he got there. Neutralizing the maximum possible number of enemies was critical, but at the moment he was even more concerned with learning what had happened to Louisa Escobar, discovering if she was still alive and helping her escape.

The service entrance to the Ramos hardsite faced a long four-car garage directly opposite. A gunner was on duty there when Johnny made the scene, his opposition startled for an instant but recovering swiftly, bringing up the stubby Heckler & Koch MP-5K submachine gun that he carried at his side.

Johnny got there first with his assault rifle, triggering a spiral burst that swept the sentry off his feet and slammed him back against the garage door, leaving crimson tracks as he slid to earth. No other lookouts were visible, and from the sound of firing out front he guessed that most or all of them were otherwise engaged.

He turned to face the door just as a loud explosion rocked the house. His brother, blasting through, and Johnny wished him well before he made his own assault, striking the service door with a solid kick that slammed it backward, showing him a pantry and the kitchen just beyond.

No one stood in his way as he shouldered through. He crossed the empty kitchen to another door, this time entering a formal dining room with seating for approximately twenty guests. Nobody home at present, and he cursed beneath his breath at having come this far without a solid contact.

No Louisa. No Sylvester Ramos.

Nothing.

Sudden gunfire erupted deeper in the house, and Johnny left Mack to it. He was doubling back to check a nearly hidden flight of stairs that he'd passed on entering. If nothing else, he might find something—someone—on the second floor. Perhaps a soldier who could tell him where Louisa was, or whether she was still alive.

In fact, he met them on the stairs, two gunners coming down, surprised as hell to meet a stranger dressed in camouflage fatigues and carrying an M-16A1. The shooter on Johnny's left was carrying an Uzi, while his sidekick had a riot shotgun. Neither one of them got off a shot before the younger Bolan raked them with a burst of 5.56 mm tumblers, blowing them away.

As one body tumbled past him on the stairs, Johnny had to leap aside to keep from being toppled off his feet. The other lay where he'd fallen, eyes open, chest fluttering weakly as he struggled to breathe.

Johnny checked behind him, saw the roller lying in a heap, head twisted at an awkward angle that could only mean a broken neck. He wrote the dead man off and turned to his companion, kneeling on the stairs to check the second gunner's pulse.

Weak and fading fast, but there it was.

"The woman!" Johnny snapped. "Where is she?"

The hardman's lips moved weakly, more a hiss than any recognizable words emerging from the gunner's throat. Johnny leaned closer.

"Again!"

And this time he got it.

"Fuck yourself, gringo!"

With a final rasp and rattle he was gone, the body slumping into death. Johnny stood and checked the stairs before he started climbing once again. He was no better off in terms of information than he'd been at the start.

But he wouldn't give up until he found Louisa one way or the other.

THE SHOTGUN BLAST missed Bolan by perhaps a foot, peppering the wall behind him. He was on the move before his adversary had an opportunity to fire again, rolling into dubious cover behind a long sofa upholstered in leather. Heavy padding and a stout wooden frame absorbed the second charge of buckshot, but he couldn't count on furniture to protect him indefinitely.

Lying on his back, Bolan reloaded the M-203 launcher with another high-explosive round, bracing himself for the move that could either make or break his game. He had no clear fix on the gunman, somewhere on the second-floor landing, but the blast radius of his grenade would allow for some marginal error if he placed it properly.

And that was the problem.

Coming out of cover under fire, he'd have about a second—maybe two—in which to make the shot. If he was slow or awkward in the execution of his move, the gunner would be waiting for him, ready and able to pick him off from a superior vantage point.

He needed a diversion to help shave the odds, but there was nothing ready at hand to assist him. Thinking fast, he drew his combat knife, slit the leather backing of the sofa, peeled a foot-square section and began to drag out the stuffing. He knew that reinforcements could arrive at any moment, rush him and blow him away before his desperate plan bore fruit. The knowledge made him work a little faster, ripping at the sofa springs until he pulled one free.

It wasn't fancy—stuffing and the twisted spring wrapped up in leather, tucked in corners skewered by the knife—but with any luck it would provide enough distraction for his needs. It all came down to timing, and he knew that he'd still be working on a heartbeat's margin, with little or nothing to spare.

He pitched the squarish bundle overhand, a lobbing pitch that caught the gunner's eye and prompted him to fire on instinct, heedless of the fact that his target was inanimate. Bolan moved at the sound of the shotgun blast, lurching out of cover in the opposite direction, leveling his launcher and squeezing off without time to aim, ducking back as the sniper saw him and spun to correct his mistake.

The explosion was jarring, confined as it was indoors, with shrapnel ripping into walls and ceiling, setting off a rain of plaster dust. Bolan rolled out of cover again and came to his knees with the rifle at his shoulder, tracking through the pall of smoke.

His target was reeling, still upright but losing it, clutching the shotgun with one hand while the other screened a bloody face. Alive meant dangerous, and Bolan remedied the situation with a short burst from the M-16A1, which slammed the gunner over on his back, feet twitching for an instant before he lay still.

Time to go, and he was halfway up the smoky stairs when voices challenged him from the ground floor, two shooters bursting through a separate entrance to the parlor, squeezing off wild rounds from their handguns. Bolan pivoted to meet them with a blazing figure eight and dumped them both in a heap, their arms and legs entwined as if embracing at the final moment of their lives.

Outside, the noise of automatic fire had escalated, battering the house, but the explosive sounds of Bolan's passage would undoubtedly attract more soldiers if anyone could be spared from the defense of the perimeter. He recognized the danger of his own exposed position and kept moving, past the dead man on the landing, turning down a corridor with bedrooms opening off either side.

No sign of life from where he stood, but he'd have to check each room in turn to make sure no one had been overlooked. A nagging sense of dread, of something missed, was gnawing at the back of Bolan's mind. His instinct told him that Louisa Escobar wouldn't be found in any of these rooms, but if he turned his back without making the effort . . .

An armed figure stood at the far end of the hall. Bolan and the new arrival saw each other at the same instant, each man crouching and prepared to fire on instinct, only holding back as recognition came.

His brother.

"More stairs this way," Johnny called, staying where he was. There might be gunmen hidden in the bedrooms yet, and neither warrior was prepared to move along the corridor without a check of each door on the way.

They had a choice to make, and Bolan knew it would be a waste of effort for both of them to search the same floor. They still had too much ground to cover as it was.

"I'll take this," Johnny told him, "if you want to finish up downstairs."

"I'll see you soon."

"Damn right."

Another pair of shooters entered the parlor as he got there, and this time Bolan had the high ground, taking both of them with measured bursts while they were gaping at the carnage spread before them.

He reloaded on the way downstairs, ditching the empty magazine and slapping a fresh one in place. No sign of Ramos or the woman yet, but he hadn't run out of hiding places. They were bound to be here somewhere, but he knew that time was running out.

And Bolan wondered if he would find either one of them alive.

IT WAS A SHIT JOB going in, Lassiter thought, and things were only getting worse. With Grissom on his heels and Harvey bringing up the rear he reached the foyer of the big house just in time to see the broad front windows shatter, raining glass in jagged sheets while bullets from an automatic weapon tracked across the inner walls.

They were catching hell from somebody, and Lassiter was stuck dead in the middle. It was all he needed, being found here with his two subordinates when someone finally called the riot squad to come and find out what the hell was going on with all the noise. He saw his twenty years go up in smoke and knew there was only one course left for him to follow.

He was bailing out, damn right, and if Sylvester Ramos didn't like it, he could fuck himself until hell froze over.

"Back this way," Lassiter snapped, his two companions looking grateful when they saw he was retreating toward the dining room and kitchen. There were several exits from the house, and the lieutenant had scoped them out on two prior visits.

"If we're lucky, we can make the car."

"If we were lucky," Grissom said, "we wouldn't be here."

"Save it, Bob. I know we're in the shit, but whining won't help anybody."

They made the kitchen, pistols drawn and ready, breezing through the pantry unopposed. He said a silent prayer of thanks for the hellacious action going down out front, a perfect draw to clear the way for anyone escaping through the rear.

But they'd have to pass along the driveway on the way out. They were using Grissom's private car, so no damage to department property if they took hits along the way. If they were forced to ditch it afterward, it would be worth the price to keep their names from coming up in an official probe.

The service door stood open, swinging in a gentle breeze that blew up from the canyon. The lock was shattered from a forced entry, but evidence meant nothing to Lassiter at the moment. Whoever had passed this way was long gone, from all appearances, no doubt engaged in battle somewhere toward the front of the house or on the floor above.

From where he stood on the threshold Lassiter could see their waiting car no more than thirty feet away. It seemed undamaged at the moment, but the rising sounds

of automatic fire told him they couldn't count on it to
stay that way for long.

"You've got the key?"

"Right here," Grissom replied, showing him.

"Okay, let's do it."

Lassiter broke for the car, feeling the others behind
him as he ran. He circled around to the passenger's side,
whipped open the door and threw himself into the shotgun seat. Grissom was behind the wheel a heartbeat later,
Harvey tumbling into the back with a breathless curse.

"Come on, haul ass!"

The engine roared to life, acceleration pressing Lassiter back into his seat. Ahead of them he saw a swirl of
smoke and running figures, gunners firing at the house,
a scattering of bodies on the lawn and driveway. Veering
hard around a limousine, Grissom fought the loss of
traction on grass, about to regain the paved driveway
when a gunner leaped in front of them, his AK-47 laying
down a screen of fire.

The windshield exploded in Lassiter's face, and something struck his chest with the force of a hammer blow.
Beside him Grissom lost it with a strangled cry of pain.
The car veered out of control, Harvey shouting something incoherent from the rear, and Lassiter had a blurred
vision of a stout oak tree rushing to meet them.

The lieutenant braced himself as best he could, legs
going numb already, but the impact pitched him forward, face first toward the shattered windshield.

And there wasn't even time to scream.

LOUISA WAS WAITING when Ramos appeared, crouching
naked in her corner of the basement, listening to the explosive sounds of combat overhead. At one point dust
had filtered down upon her head, the floor vibrating vi-

olently, and she'd worried that the house might be on fire, trapping her in her cell. She'd considered mounting the stairs, trying to force the door on her own, but it seemed hopeless without some tool or weapon at hand.

Her body ached from the abusive treatment she had suffered, burns from the electric contact points along with sundry cuts and bruises, but her real discomfort came from having broken down, providing Ramos with the information he required to get in touch with Johnny Gray. If something happened to the lawyer—or to Pablo—it would be her fault, a grievous error she'd have no chance to correct in this life.

The sound of Ramos coming down the stairs brought Louisa a new tremor of fear, but it also gave her fresh hope. The dealer might have come to finish her off, in which case there was nothing she could do... but, on the other hand, he might still need her for some reason. She had no idea what all the shooting meant, except that Ramos must be catching hell from someone.

Whoever it was, she wished them luck.

Ramos crossed the open concrete floor to where she sat, covering Louisa with an automatic pistol, dangling a khaki shirt in his free hand. He tossed it at her, standing back and watching while she turned away and slipped it on, buttoning the shirt with trembling hands.

"Get up."

She struggled to her feet, ignoring the stiffness and pain in her legs, taking a moment to get her balance.

"What's going on?" she asked.

"An act of treachery. You will join me, Sergeant. Just in case I need you later. Think of yourself as my passport, if you like."

"I'd like to see you burn in hell," she spit.

"Perhaps another time. This way."

She followed his direction, moving toward the stairs and climbing slowly, taking her time, conscious of the pistol at her back. She thought about a kick to knock the weapon from his hand, but she couldn't be certain where Ramos was without turning around, thus telegraphing her move. And if she missed, well, there would be no second chance before he cut her down.

"Be quick about it!" Ramos ordered, slapping at her flank.

Louisa picked up her pace a little, moving toward the door. A few more steps and she would reach the pantry. Once across the threshold...

Sudden inspiration gripped her as she reached the doorway. Lunging through, she grasped the door and whipped it shut behind her, slamming it in the dealer's face. She heard him curse, a bullet ripping through the panel to her left, and then she was running for her life, caroming off the pantry shelves and breaking for the yard outside.

Behind her Ramos breached the door and bellowed out for her to stop, another bullet whining past her head. The grass was cool and moist beneath her naked feet.

Louisa ran for her life, with grim death closing on her heels.

BOLAN LEFT THE HOUSE as he had entered, through the shattered sliding doors, across the patio. A dead man was floating in the swimming pool, surrounded by a spreading slick of blood. Two other corpses huddled on the deck, unmoving where they'd fallen when they were shot. Thirty yards across the lawn a car was burning, laying down a heavy screen of smoke, its front end crumpled against a shade tree. Around the front of the building the sounds of battle had begun to falter, but he couldn't say which side was winning out.

Nor did he care.

His downstairs search, avoiding contact with Ramos's gunners where he could, had turned up nothing that would put him on the dealer's track or show him where Louisa Escobar was being held. As Bolan circled toward the rear of the house, a runner exploded from the service entrance, breaking toward the garage and cliff beyond. Long, flashing legs were exposed beneath the tails of a khaki work shirt, and Bolan recognized Louisa Escobar in profile.

A shot exploded behind her, and Ramos lurched into Bolan's line of sight, shouting after the woman as he lined up another shot. It was the first time he'd seen the dealer in the flesh, but there was no mistaking him from Johnny's mug shots.

"Ramos!"

The dealer faltered in midstride, spinning to face Bolan with his automatic braced in both hands, locking into target acquisition. Shock and sudden curiosity froze his finger on the weapon's trigger, a strange expression twisting his face.

"Who the hell are you?"

"Does it matter?"

"The Escalante brothers send you?"

"No one had to send me, Ramos. You're deserving on your own."

"So now what?"

"Now you say goodbye."

"How about I say, 'Fuck you!'"

He telegraphed the move, arms tightening into the squeeze, and Bolan beat him to it with the 40 mm launcher, triggering an HE round from forty feet away.

The flash eclipsed his target for a moment, smoke and fire, before he saw his target airborne, arms and legs spinning in a boneless cartwheel. Ramos hit the ground like a sack of old laundry, limp and unmoving, his spine twisted at an unnatural angle.

Bolan turned and found Louisa staring at him with a dazed expression on her face. A sudden flash of recognition brightened her eyes.

"Can we get out of here?" she asked him, a tremor in her voice.

"We're still one short."

"Not anymore," Johnny said, stepping through the service entrance where the woman and Ramos had emerged moments earlier.

A new explosion rocked the house, and in the distance they could hear a rising wail of sirens, drawing closer by the moment.

"Same way we came?" Johnny asked.

"Might as well." Bolan glanced at Louisa's bare feet. "You'll need some shoes."

She swallowed hard and moved to stand beside Ramos, crouching as she began to tug at his boots.

"This bastard owes me one," she said. "His feet are bigger than his brain, but what the hell."

A moment later she was ready, waiting for them as the Executioner struck off and led them toward the cliff. They had a long way back, and questions left unanswered if they made it in one piece, but they were on their way.

And getting there was half the battle, right?

EPILOGUE

"You mean it's that simple?" Louisa asked. She was working on her second glass of wine, enjoying it, and it was showing in her voice.

"I wouldn't call it simple," Johnny answered, "but it works. The bishop knew about Father Marcos, of course, and he's agreed to take care of Pablo without involving the authorities. They'll be in touch across the border to try to locate any family. If nothing works out over there, the church has a program that should cover it."

"You're sure?"

"I'm sure. I've done some prior work with the bishop on his Central American amnesty program. It wouldn't be the first time paperwork fell through the cracks in a good cause."

"And Pablo won't be called to testify?"

"To what?" Bolan asked, facing her across the coffee table, sipping at his beer. "With Ramos, Lassiter and his playmates out of the picture, there's no one to prosecute for the killings. As far as the small-fry are concerned, they're going up on weapons charges, drug possession, unrelated murder counts. The boy couldn't help with that, even if he wanted to."

"I guess we caught a break with Lassiter and the others turning up to visit Ramos," Louisa said.

"I'd say."

The sheriff's officers had been identified from finger-prints and dental records after roasting in their car. Clean sweep.

"One thing," Louisa said. "I still don't know exactly who or what you are."

"What difference does it make?"

She hesitated, frowning, finally turning it around into a cautious smile. "None, I guess. That is, unless you plan on hanging out in San Diego regularly. I'm still working homicide, remember?"

"I remember. I'm out of here tomorrow morning at the latest."

"As for you..."

She turned to Johnny, Bolan noticing that her smile had transformed itself, becoming something else entirely.

"Me?" The younger Bolan grinned disarmingly. "I'm back in court on Thursday, soon as I shake this touch of the flu."

"I just may have to keep my eye on you," the sergeant told him.

"If you must."

Bolan rose, taking his beer with him, moving toward the Strongbase kitchen and its telephone.

"I've got some calls to make," he said. "You two don't mind?"

"We'll get along."

Bolan checked his watch. It would be dinnertime in Washington, Brognola sitting down with his wife if he was lucky, if nothing critical had intervened to spoil his evening.

This call, anyway, would bring some good news for a change. A job completed, loose ends neatly tied around the proper necks to form a hangman's noose.

And if Brognola had another job on tap for Bolan back to back, well, that was fine.

He knew that any respite from the hellgrounds was a temporary thing at best. His life lay on the firing line, and it had been his choice. No turning back.

The savages were waiting for him, right.

The Executioner wouldn't have had it any other way.

Gold Eagle brings another fast-paced miniseries to the action adventure front!

by PATRICK F. ROGERS

Omega Force: the last—and deadliest—option

With capabilities unmatched by any other paramilitary organization in the world, Omega Force is a special ready-reaction antiterrorist strike force composed of the best commandos and equipment the military has to offer.

In Book 1: **WAR MACHINE**, two dozen SCUDs have been smuggled into Libya by a secret Iraqi extremist group whose plan is to exact ruthless retribution in the Middle East. The President has no choice but to call in Omega Force—a swift and lethal way to avert World War III.

Take
4 explosive books
plus a
mystery bonus
FREE

Mail to: Gold Eagle Reader Service
3010 Walden Ave.,
P.O. Box 1394
Buffalo, NY 14240-1394

YEAH! Rush me 4 FREE Gold Eagle novels and my FREE mystery gift. Then send me
4 brand-new novels every other month as they come off the presses. Bill me at the low
price of just $13.80* for each shipment—a saving of over 10% off the cover prices for all
four books! There is NO extra charge for postage and handling! There is no minimum
number of books I must buy. I can always cancel at any time simply by returning a
shipment at your cost or by returning any shipping statement marked "cancel." Even if I
never buy another book from Gold Eagle, the 4 free books and surprise gift are mine to
keep forever.   164 BPM AEQ6

_____
Name   (PLEASE PRINT)

_____
Address   Apt. No.

_____
City   State   Zip

_____
Signature (if under 18, parent or guardian must sign)

*Terms and prices subject to change without notice. Sales tax applicable in NY. This offer
is limited to one order per household and not valid to present subscribers. Offer not
available in Canada.

© 1991 GOLD EAGLE   AC-92R